P9-BYM-062

"Harry?" she whispered. "You are alive? Truly?"

"So I have always believed, my love, but I have never been so glad of it as at this moment."

Kate choked on a joyful sob and struggled to rise. But in the delirium of her joy, she quite forgot that she was a bishop's daughter. She tipped back her head, eagerly seeking his lips. Harry's eyes widened, but his noble resistance lasted no more than a second. If he was dreaming, he thought, leaning over Kate for another kiss, he did not want to be awakened. Too late did he see the unaccustomed flash of fire in her eyes, the blur of her hand as she struck out, soundly boxing his ears.

"You—you heartless beast," Kate cried. "You unfeeling monster . . ."

Also by Susan Carroll
Published by Fawcett Books:

THE LADY WHO HATED SHAKESPEARE
THE SUGAR ROSE
BRIGHTON ROAD

THE BISHOP'S DAUGHTER

Susan Carroll

FAWCETT CREST • NEW YORK

A Fawcett Crest Book
Published by Ballantine Books
Copyright © 1990 by Susan Coppula

All rights reserved under International and Pan-American Copyright Conventions. Published in the United States by Ballantine Books, a division of Random House, Inc., New York, and simultaneously in Canada by Random House of Canada Limited, Toronto.

Library of Congress Catalog Card Number: 90-90297

ISBN 0-449-21693-4

Manufactured in the United States of America

First Edition: November 1990

Chapter 1

Lord Harcourt Arundel never expected a hero's welcome, even though he had been wounded at Waterloo. As he trudged along the lane, leading his dun-colored gelding by the reins, his portmanteau strapped back of the saddle, he felt neither particularly lordly nor heroic. His top boots, buckskins, and frock coat caked with dust, his sun-bronzed features streaked with sweat, what Lord Harry felt was tired.

Still, after a year's absence from his Northamptonshire estate, he would have thought there might be at least one face to smile upon him, someone to bob a curtsy by way of greeting to the returning Earl of Lytton. Yet the only soul stirring was a mongrel dog panting in the shade of the hedgerows, too affected by the heat radiating from the August sun to even bark.

Shading eyes the hue of hunter's green, Lord Harry peered across the empty expanse of his fields, the tall waves of rye but half-cut, the grain corded in neat bundles waiting to be loaded upon the wagons.

Harry frowned, his thick brows as startlingly black as the lustrous waves of his hair. "Where the deuce is everyone?" he muttered.

He had never paid half the attention that he should have to the farming operations on his own land, but even he knew how crucial it was to bring in the rye as soon as it had ripened. Yet the fields bore that tranquil Sunday kind of stillness, although it was near noon of a Saturday.

" 'Twould seem they all heard Hellfire Harry was coming back and took to their heels, eh Ramses?" Lord Harry said, reaching up to pat his horse's neck. Though still puzzled, the frown that was so foreign to Harry's countenance faded to his customary easy smile as he reflected that the only one likely to retreat at his approach would be his stepmother.

His unheralded return would undoubtedly give Sybil a megrim. His presence had been doing so ever since he was seven and first introduced to his new mama, and the condition had not abated a jot these past twenty years.

"Oh, Harry," the Dowager Countess of Lytton would be sure to exclaim, reaching for her smelling salts with a shudder. "You—you look so hale. So robust."

How or why his unfailing good health invariably made his stepmother feel ill, Harry had never been able to fathom. He merely accepted the fact with the philosophical cheerfulness he treated all his fellow creatures' foibles.

The same spirit of tolerance caused him to spare only one more glance for his deserted fields, the obvious evidence of his steward's neglect. Then with a shrug of his broad shoulders, he tugged at Ramses's reins and marched on. The movement, slight as it was, caused a pain to shoot along Harry's left arm.

That shoulder but two months ago had played host to a chunk of shrapnel from a mortar exploding near him in the very thick of battle. The army surgeon had said the wound had healed remarkably well, but he had warned Harry to take the journey home in easy stages.

Harry never did anything in easy stages. Even

now he felt more concern for his horse than himself. Ramses had picked up a stone just outside the village of Lytton's Dene. Although Harry had managed to remove it, the soft portion of Ramses's hoof remained bruised and tender.

As he led the halting animal, he murmured words of encouragement, "Not much further now, old fellow. We'll soon have a poultice slapped on that hoof and after a few days' rest, you'll be fit to go."

Harry hoped he would not have to lead the horse the entire way round the park to the drive winding up to Mapleshade Hall, his principal country seat. The stone fence at the back of the park had ever been a crumbling ruin, and Harry trusted that no one would have seen fit to repair it in his absence.

His trust was not misplaced. As the fields sloped away to become woodland, Harry saw that the stonework, far from being repaired, had eroded a little further. There was no difficulty about leading Ramses through the break, thus shortening the journey to the stable by at least half a mile.

And it was not as if anyone up at the hall would be looking out eagerly for Harry's return. Not with his own father dead these past six years. There would be no one to reproach him for not making haste to enter the house. It might have been entirely another matter if Miss Kathryn Towers had returned him a different answer to a certain question. . . .

Harry expelled a faint sigh as he led his horse deeper into the shadows of the timberland. He had not meant to think of Kate. The dappled light filtering through the trees' foliage faded as memory misted before his eyes. Two years had passed since that spring, yet he could still envision Kate so clearly, the warm breeze teasing the dusky locks of her hair, the fragile flowers being unconsciously plucked apart by her slender white fingers as she stood with her back to him. She had looked so soft, so vulnerable, all of a woman with none of the primness of the Bishop of Chillingsworth's daughter about her.

"I don't expect you to understand, Harry," she had said in the low musical voice of hers, "any of the reasons why I cannot marry you."

It was then he should have summoned up all the eloquence and persuasiveness at his command. God knows he could be glib enough upon all other occasions. Why, when he wanted to be tender, did the words seem to form a lump at the base of his throat? He had swallowed that lump and said in teasing tones, "It will do you no good, Kate, to stand there, wreaking havoc upon those poor flowers. I shan't take no for an answer. You shall never be rid of me until you can look me in the eye and tell me you don't love me."

Gripping her shoulders, he had forced her to come about and face him, intending to express all that he could not say with the warmth of his kiss. But she had stiffened and he had felt a tremor pass through her. After a heartbeat of hesitation, she had gazed upon him, her eyes so steady, so clear, the same vivid shade as the violets tumbling heedlessly from her hands. His Kate was gone. It was the bishop's daughter who answered him.

"I don't love you, my lord."

Remembrance of those words pierced Harry with a sharp ache, but no bitterness. Never had he ever felt any bitterness toward Kate, only a sense of longing, a melancholy that sometimes he could shrug off with a quick laugh and sometimes he couldn't.

As he tromped through the woods, each step taking him closer to the empty grandeur of Mapleshade, he felt more than usually prey to gloom and was glad when a diversion occurred to banish Kate's image from his mind.

The sharp crackling of a twig alerted Harry that he was no longer alone. He glanced up eagerly. After the unnatural quiet of the fields, he thought that he would be glad of the sight of any familiar face, even if it should prove to be only Jergens, his dour gameskeeper.

But the sprightly little man who came slipping through the bracken was not Jergens. Balancing a wriggling brown sack upon his shoulder, the shrewd-featured fellow paused to glance over his shoulder, the hairs of his thick red beard seeming to bristle like the fur of a fox scenting pursuit.

Harry's mouth widened to a grin as he recognized Tim Keegan. An itinerant Irish laborer hired on for the extra work at the harvest every summer, the rogue had a habit of "borrowing" hares from his lordship's coveys. Judging from the movement of the sack, Keegan must have snared himself a plump one this time.

Intent upon peering behind him for any sign of the gameskeeper, Keegan took no note of Lord Harry. Regarding the little man's furtive movements with amusement, Harry folded his arms across his chest and waited until Keegan had all but backed into Ramses.

"Halloo, Keegan," Harry said.

The soft greeting nearly caused the Irishman to shoot out of his boots. As his startled gaze fell upon Harry, Keegan's eyes bulged. All color drained from his florid features. He dropped the sack and crossed himself with a loud wail. "Sweet holy Mary, Mother of God defend me."

"Steady on, old man. I never intended to give you that much of a fright." Harry gave Keegan a bracing clap on the shoulder, but far from reassuring the man, it caused Keegan to shrink away, flinging up one hand as though to ward off a blow.

"Saints above! I'll be after putting the rabbit back straightaway, that I will. Just don't be a-haunting me, yer lardship."

Haunting him? What was the fool talking about? Keegan took a sidestep, preparing to bolt. Harry prevented him by catching hold of his coattails.

"What is the matter with you, Keegan?" Securing a firm grip on the man's trembling arm, Harry brought him about, demanding, "Now when have I ever cut up stiff over a plaguey rabbit? I only want to ask you a few questions."

"Questions!" From Keegan's terrified howl, he might have been about to face the Spanish Inquisition.

"Why aren't you at work in the fields? And where is everyone else? I have not seen a soul since passing by the crossroads to the village."

"They—they all be gived the ar'ternoon off to have a look at the memorial an' it please yer worship."

"Memorial? What memorial? Who has died?"

"Why . . . why, *yerself*, me lard."

Keegan's doleful reply startled Harry so much, he released the Irishman.

"Myself?" Harry repeated. Keegan had either had a spot too much of the sun or had been tippling the usquebaugh again. Harry chuckled. "I suppose at the moment I do look like something that has just crept from the grave, and I am nigh dead with fatigue, but—"

"Oh, no. Beggin' yer lardship's pardon," Keegan interrupted tremulously. "Ye must have forgotten. It wasn't fatigue as took yer lardship off, but a great nasty cannonball as smashed off yer head."

His words carried such conviction that Harry had to suppress an urge to touch his own head to make certain it was still affixed to his shoulders.

"Where did you come by such a rum tale as that?" he asked.

" 'Twas yer good vicar Thorpe, me lard."

The vicar? Harry grimaced. That, at least, explained Timothy Keegan's belief that he must be

6

seeing a shade from the other world. Any utterance made by Harry's cousin, the most holy Reverend Adolphus Thorpe was regarded in the village as being a pronouncement from God, even by a Catholic like Keegan.

"You can plainly see that I am not dead," Harry said. "You must have misunderstood what Reverend Thorpe told you."

"Did I indeed, soor?" Keegan asked, keeping a wary distance between himself and Harry. "Then what about the memorial and the deddycashun this ar-ternoon?"

"The deddy-what?"

"Deddycashun. 'Tis my understandin' 'tis to be sort of a wake for yer lardship, only without the food and drink, which doesn't make it much of a wake a'tall to my way of thinkin'." Keegan fixed Harry with a pitying gaze. "Shabby, I calls it. Ye might as well not even have died."

"But I didn't—" Harry broke off, torn between amusement and exasperation at the absurdity of the conversation. Exhausted as he was and eager to get Ramses to the stable, he did not know why he was stopping to bandy words with this madman. Perhaps it was because the mystery of his empty fields yet remained, and Keegan was so adamant about the memorial.

Was it possible that some ridiculous mistake had occurred and everyone else at Mapleshade also presumed Harry to be— No, impossible!

True, he had taken no pains to communicate with his family since Waterloo, but plenty of his returning comrades knew he was not dead. And the British Army certainly knew it had been no ghost captain who had recently sold his commission. There was no reason that any false report could have been carried back to his home.

Having convinced himself that this was so, Harry

7

could not say why he still felt uneasy. Nor why, instead of pursuing his course toward the stables, he turned to Keegan and said, "Perhaps you had better be showing me this memorial."

The superstitious Keegan did not evince much enthusiasm for accompanying one he persisted in viewing as a ghost. But after Harry had pressed a guinea into his hand and told him he might keep the rabbit besides, Keegan cheerfully declared he would be willing to guide the devil himself under such terms.

"Yer ever as generous a man dead as ye were alive, me lard." Keegan beamed, retrieving the sack. "The memorial be right this way, atop the Hill."

Biting back a smile, Harry followed him, although with this information, he scarce had need of Keegan any longer. In this gently rolling section of Northamptonshire, there was only one slope hereabouts that merited the name, the Hill, being a part of Harry's own parklands. It had ever been Harry's favorite spot those rare times he desired solitude. From the summit, he could gaze down upon his own woods, the lily-bedecked pond, the grassy expanse where deer often grazed, even the distant chimneys of the hall itself. It had been to the Hill that he had retreated as a lad when his favorite pony had broken its leg and had to be destroyed, there, as a man, that he had gone when his father had died, there that he had brought Kate to ask her to be his bride, there that she had refused.

As the tree line thinned and he and Keegan emerged from the shelter of the trees, Harry expected to find his Hill as ever, green, quiet, undisturbed.

He was brought up short by the mass of humanity swarming over it. Only yards ahead of him were his missing farm laborers, mingling with what appeared to be the better part of the villagers from Lytton's Dene. Heavy boots trampled the daisies underfoot, while homespun skirts brushed the grass. This group kept a respectful distance from the denizens of Mapleshade, those servants who staffed Harry's stables and the massive hall itself. At the head of these, Harry could make out the forms of some silk-clad ladies and gentlemen, among them, his nearest neighbors, the portly Squire Gresham and his lady; his own stepmother garbed in deepest mourning; and his cousins, the stately, beautiful Julia Thorpe and her brother, the vicar.

The sunlight gleamed off Adolphus's fair hair as, like an anxious shepherd, that reverend gentleman assembled this rather mixed flock at the Hill's summit where stood some massive, mysterious object draped with canvas.

"Good God!" Harry breathed, no longer able to deny the significance of the scene before him. "It would seem you are right, Mr. Keegan," he said dryly. "I *am* dead."

"Wasn't I after tellin' yer lardship so."

Harry could only shake his head, still unable to fathom how such a ridiculous misunderstanding could have happened. Nor how this gathering on the hillside had come about.

"Why didn't they just hold the service down in the church?" he mused aloud. "I know Adolphus always thought I was paving hell with a vengeance. But I can't believe that even he would refuse me the last rites."

"Oh, nay, me lard. They had you a proper church service, so they did. But this memorial, I heerd tell, was your stepmama's notion, herself wantin' all to remember what a hero ye were."

Harry felt both surprised and touched by this gesture on Sybil's part until Keegan added, "An' it gave her a wonderful chance to throw a dab of work in the way of her friend, Mr. Crosbie."

Harry stiffened at the mention of Lucillus Crosbie, a would-be sculptor. Man-milliner and fortune hunter were two of the kinder epithets Harry had bestowed upon the man. The last time he had been home, a year ago, he had caught Crosbie making sheep's eyes at his stepmother and had introduced the impertinent fellow to the fish at the bottom of Mapleshade's pond. Harry had thought to have seen the last of him. Apparently Lucillus had wasted little time reinstating himself into Sybil's graces when Harry had been reported dead.

Thrusting Ramses's reins at Keegan, Harry bade him look after the horse. "Much as I hate to disappoint everyone," he said. "I am afraid I must announce that I am so inconsiderate as to still be alive."

With that, Harry strode forward from the shelter of the trees and began to mount the Hill. He did not check his step until he reached the fringes of the crowd. It suddenly occurred to him that he might be about to cause consternation to others as he had Keegan by thus announcing his return from the dead. Yet glancing at the rapt expressions about him, Harry believed he could have dressed in a bedsheet and howled like a banshee without attracting attention. All eyes were riveted on Reverend Thorpe.

Harry suspected that most of those about him had attended less to pay final respects than out of curiosity. Harry certainly did not blame them for that. He was curious as hell himself as to what monstrosity of Crosbie's lay concealed beneath that canvas.

As he skirted the crowd, advancing ever higher up the Hill, the sound of the vicar's piercing voice began to carry to him in snatches. His cousin appeared to be delivering some sort of eulogy.

"And I trust that our dear Lord Lytton is at this moment enjoying all the blisses of heaven."

Harry grinned for he knew full well that the righteous Adolphus was mentally consigning his wicked cousin to the hottest of flames. Reverend Thorpe's speech became even more disjointed as he tried to enumerate Harry's many virtues and was apparently having difficulty thinking of any.

At last the Reverend blurted out, "Er—a most godly man, an example to the entire community."

Harry, who by this time had arrived behind the squire, within a stone's throw of the monument, nearly choked. *Godly?* He, who had never seen the inside of a church since his christening day? And even then he had been carried screaming into the vestibule.

Harry saw that he had best step forward at once and save his cousin the embarrassment of coming out with any more such plumpers. But before he could edge past the squire's bulky frame, the vicar turned, stretching up one hand toward the canvas.

The crowd collectively held its breath as the vicar intoned, "This solemn edifice has been erected by a grieving mother to the memory of the most generous and affectionate of sons, a brave and bold hero whose life has been so tragically cut short. But with this likeness mounted upon the Hill, Lord Harcourt Andrew Stephen Arundel, the fifth Earl of Lytton, will dwell among us forever."

As the canvas came away, Harry expected to see some awful representation of himself in stone, garbed in full military dress in one of those stiff unnatural poses. As he gazed upward, he was as confounded as the rest of the assemblage. Mounted upon a plinth, rising to a full seven feet of glory, stood the muscular figure of man carved in Classical fashion, his tightly curling hair in nowise resembling Harry's own straight locks. But no one paid much heed to the head for the statue had been carved stark naked. Only the modest manner in which the figure held a sword before him prevented the full disclosure of his manhood.

A stunned hush fell over the crowd, then many of

the women present let out shocked and delighted shrieks, while the men exclaimed.

"Damnation," the squire roared.

"Abomination!" The outraged vicar staggered back as though he had uncovered the devil himself.

"Exquisite," the Dowager Lady Lytton cooed, dabbing at her plump face with a black-edged handkerchief, taking pains not to mar the layering of paint meant to conceal her fifty-odd years.

"Ridiculous!" said the squire's thin wife. "It looks nothing like Lord Harry. He was never so thick about the waist, and I am sure he had a much finer set of legs—"

"Upon my word, madam." The squire leveled his wife an awful stare. "You seem to have made a thorough study of the matter."

Mrs. Gresham colored. "It is nothing that any woman . . . er . . . that is— Anyone who knew his lordship would say the same."

By this time, Harry feared the only mourner present with tears glistening in his eyes was himself as he struggled to contain his mirth. But as his gaze chanced upon his cousin Julia, affecting to look so prim, so disapproving, all the while she kept stealing glances upward at the statue's firmly muscled buttocks, it became entirely too much for Harry's self-control. He burst into a roar of laughter that seemed to ring all the more loudly amid the astonished silence of the crowd.

Indignant faces turned toward him only to go pale with recognition. Through his peals of mirth, he heard the gasps, his name rippling through the crowd like a rush of wind through the willows. His stepmother let out a piercing cry and clutched at her heart. The Reverend Thorpe so far forgot himself as to take the name of the Lord in vain.

Harry tried to speak, but couldn't. He could only glance helplessly about him, wishing he could find at least one other kindred spirit to share this moment, someone else who could see the humor of the situation.

Instead he encountered a face that drove the laughter from his lips, the last face in the world he had expected to encounter. Standing close to his shoulder was a solemn-looking lady garbed in pearl gray, so close that he wondered how he could have missed her before.

Harry experienced a shock not unlike the one he had felt when blasted from his saddle at Waterloo. He stared into violet eyes that registered a mingling of disbelief, joy, and reproach.

"Kate!" Harry cried hoarsely.

Kate's lips attempted to form his name as what little color she possessed drained from her cheeks. Harry retained just enough presence of mind to open his arms wide and catch her as she swayed into a dead faint.

Chapter 2

Miss Kathryn Towers had nearly decided not to attend the dedication of Lord Lytton's memorial. An hour before the ceremony was scheduled to begin, she had lingered in the parlor window seat of the cottage orné she shared with her mother in the village of Lytton's Dene.

It was unusual for Kate to sit idle for so long, staring vacantly out the window, but that is what she had been doing, her gaze fixing upon the elder bushes growing just beneath the latticed panes, their white blossoms thick among the greenery like a scattering of summer snow.

Snow . . . Would she ever be able to think of it again without also thinking of Harry? It had been winter when he had first come crashing, quite literally into her life, that last winter when Papa had still been alive. A sad, half smile tipped Kate's lips.

She had been bundled up in a fur-lined cloak, strolling in the garden of the Episcopal Palace at Chillingsworth, watching the deep blue of twilight fade to darkness. The full moon rose, shining a silvery glow over the snow-shrouded landscape, making the garden sparkle like crystal. The blanket of white had cast a hush over everything, an aura of enchantment, of expectancy as though something was about to happen. Or was that now only her imagination in looking back? For something *had* happened. . . .

A curricle had come smashing through the low-lying hedge, finishing up by knocking over the statue of John the Apostle. One wheel of the carriage broke, flinging its driver into what remained of the rose bed.

With a cry of alarm, Kate rushed forward, but the man was already climbing from the wreckage quite unperturbed, dusting snow from the torn capes of his garrick. As he went round to quiet his horse, he said, "Sorry, miss, but it was either your statue or a little urchin who slipped into the road."

"It—it was John the Apostle," Kate stammered.

"Who? The urchin?"

"No, the statue," she said solemnly.

For some reason, that made the stranger laugh. "Rather odd place to keep an apostle."

Secretly Kate agreed with him. She had always said the statue was placed far too close to the hedge, although she would not have expressed her opinion in quite the same manner.

As the moonlight outlined his profile, the thick waves of coal dark hair, the strong, stubborn jawline, she recognized who he was. Kate felt a tingling of alarm as she realized it was a most dangerous man who had invaded her garden. Even she had heard of Hellfire Harry, the wild young Earl of Lytton who frequently drove in from his estates to Chillingsworth. Not to attend services in the cathedral either, but to engage in such vulgar pursuits as attending race meets and prize fights or to carouse with his friends in one of the taverns.

But when she noticed his forehead was bleeding, all thoughts of Harry's dubious reputation had been swept from her mind. As the bishop's daughter, she had no choice but to invite him into the palace, even though the bishop was gone to read the services at evensong and her mother was away attending the confinement of one of her dearest friends.

Nor had she any choice but to see to his wound, although he would only permit her to do so after he had made sure that his horse was well cared for. As she had prepared to place sticking plaster on the cut, she found herself studying his lordship's face. He was perhaps more handsome at close range than he had appeared those times she had glimpsed him from a distance, his features, even in the winter, bearing the rugged healthy appearance of a man who spends most of his time out of doors. Kathryn had always supposed that one as reportedly wicked as Lord Lytton would bear some signs of it in his countenance, a hinting of dissipation.

But there was naught of the hardened roué about Harry's face, only a clean strength in the angular line of his jaw, an almost boyishness in the jet black strand of hair that tumbled across his forehead, mischief lurking in the most vivid green eyes Kate had ever seen.

With her parents gone, she should never have encouraged him to stay, but how could she turn an injured man from her doorstep? She asked him to partake of tea.

She could still remember how awkward his large hands had looked balancing the dainty Sevres cup, heroically screwing up his face with each sip he took. She sat upon the settee, mending the tear in his garrick, the snow softly falling outside the tall windows, the fire blazing on the hearth, the deep sound of Harry's voice rumbling pleasantly in her ears. She could not remember exactly what outrageous things he had said only that she had never smiled and blushed so much in her life.

From time to time she peeked up from her work to steal glances at him. Her father had raised her to be wary, to place no value on mere handsomeness. It was the beauties of a man's character that mattered.

But why had not the bishop seen fit to warn her how dangerous green eyes could be, eyes that crinkled at the corners when a man laughed and a smile that came so warm, so ready, so utterly disarming?

A smile that Kate could scarce bring herself to believe she would never see again. . . .

"Kate?" Her mother's voice had cut through Kate's haze of memories. Rather reluctantly, she turned to face the tiny wisp of a woman who stood regarding her. Although it had been two years since Papa's death, her mother still wore her simple black gowns, the white lace of her widow's cap most becoming to her silvery blond hair and the soft contours of her face. Maisie Towers's plain countenance bore the lines of her years, but her eyes remained the same deep violet shade as Kate's, although Kate often felt that her mother's held more of a sweetness of expression than her own.

"It is nearly past noon. You have decided not to attend the dedication after all?" Mrs. Towers asked, a hint of relief in her tones.

At that moment with Harry's memory so fresh, so poignant in her mind, Kate wished she could cry out, no, she did not wish to go. Her mourning for Harry had ever been a private matter. Indeed, she almost felt as though she was not entitled to any grief, having turned Harry away. She didn't want to attend the dedication, be expected to admire some horrid memorial. Harry had not been the kind of man whose image could be captured in cold, unfeeling stone.

When Kate took so long about answering, her mother sank down beside her on the window seat. Rather diffidently, she covered one of Kate's hands with her own.

"You don't have to go if you don't want to, Kate," Mrs. Towers said. "I could offer some excuse to the vicar's sister when she comes to call for you."

Gazing into her mother's eyes, Kate found an unexpected amount of sympathy. She wanted to cast herself into her mother's arms and burst into tears. But Mrs. Towers's health had ever been delicate. Even as a child, Kate had known she must not distress Mama with her own miseries. And indeed how could anyone as gentle and uncomplicated as her mother possibly understand the bewildering conflict of Kate's emotions about Harry? She scarce understood them herself.

Suppressing a sigh, Kate drew her hand back from her mother's comforting warmth.

"Of course, I must attend the dedication, Mama," she said. "It is my duty."

Mentally Kate scolded herself for forgetting that. She was still the bishop's daughter, and no one knew better than Kate what was expected of one in that role.

"I realize that someone of our family should attend," her mother murmured, "but perhaps I should go instead."

"Oh, no, Mama. *You* out in this heat? Unthinkable."

"I am not so fragile as you would suppose, Kate. I should gladly do it to spare you—" Her mother broke off, looking uncomfortable. "Even though we never discussed it, I could not help noticing what passed between you and Lord Harry that winter. I thought you had developed a tendre for—"

"No!" Kate cried. Appalled by her own outburst, she rose to her feet and took a nervous turn about the small, cramped parlor. Forcing a smile to her lips, she said, "You are so romantical, Mama. How could I possibly have fallen in love with a man I knew Papa would strongly disapprove of?"

"I don't suppose you could, Kate." Mrs. Towers sighed. "You were ever the most sensible girl."

Why that pronouncement should make her mother look so melancholy, Kate did not understand. She felt rather relieved when they were interrupted by a light rap on the door. The plump, pretty maid, Mollie, came bouncing into the room, nearly knocking her father's bust of Thomas à Becket from its perch atop the pianoforte.

After the spaciousness of the palace, the Towers family belongings were crowded within the cottage. Kate's pianoforte abutted so close to the bookcase containing the bishop's religious tomes that the glass doors with their elegant tracery could scarce be opened.

As Kate rushed forward in time to save Becket, Mollie dipped into a curtsy, her cap ribbons fluttering saucily behind her.

"Mollie, I have told you to take more care when entering a room," Kate said.

"Sorry, Miss Kate. I was in that much of a hurry to tell you that Miss Thorpe be waiting outside with her carriage."

"Why didn't you show her in?"

Mollie thrust her nose upward in imitation of the vicar's sister. "Miss Thorpe did not *deign* to come inside, miss."

Kate frowned. But before she could rebuke the girl, Mrs. Towers said gently, "Thank you, Mollie. That will do."

With an unrepentant grin, Mollie ducked back out of the room. Sensing that her mother intended to make one final appeal to change her mind and fearing that she might be weak enough to be persuaded, Kate also made haste. Gathering up her gloves from the window seat, she briskly put them on. Kissing her mother's cheek, she said, "I shall not be gone long, Mama. You must not worry about me."

Her mother's only reply had been a sad, wistful kind of smile.

Bustling out of the parlor, Kate paused before the pier glass in the tiny front vestibule only long enough to don her bonnet. Primping and fussing over one's appearance was the worst sort of vanity.

And it was not as though she had a great deal to fuss about, Kate thought wryly as she began to tie the satin ribbons beneath her chin in a modest bow. She was just passably pretty. Only Harry had ever said she was beautiful, but it had been one of those rare times he had not been teasing her. . . .

Kate's hands had stilled upon the ribbon. Staring at her reflection, she could find no beauty, only a quiet despair in eyes that seemed far too large for the pale oval of her face.

Averting her gaze, Kate forced her fingers back into brisk movement, finishing the bow, smoothing the tendrils of her dark ringlets already damp and curling overmuch from the heat. There was nothing wrong, she assured herself. She had been ill of late . . . the influenza. That was why she had no color.

Strange that this bout of influenza should have come upon you a month ago, a voice inside her jabbed. *About the same time you heard that Harry had been killed.*

But Kate chose to ignore the voice. With hands that trembled slightly, she retrieved her parasol from the hall stand and stepped out of the cottage's cool shelter into a hot flood of sunlight.

As she trudged down the path toward the garden gate, she stole one glance behind her. Never had the cottage with its ivy-covered walls and roof of bright green Colleystone tile seemed like such a place of refuge. If only Lady Lytton had not insisted that memorial be erected upon that same hill where she had last seen Harry. How was she ever to face the ordeal ahead of her, the rush of painful memories?

With all the dignity to be expected of the late Bishop of Chillingsworth's daughter, Kate adjured herself sternly. Squaring her shoulders, she turned, marching onward through the creaking wooden gate.

The Thorpes' barouche awaited her in the lane, the coachman patiently standing at the head of the team of bays. Kate had often heard the more spiteful among the villagers wondering why a country vicar should possess such an equipage, but as Julia Thorpe loftily reminded everyone, she and her brother *were* first cousins to an earl.

The coachman stepped forward to greet Kate and hand her into the carriage. As Kate blinked, adjusting her eyes to the coach's dark blue velvet interior, she discerned the figure of Miss Julia Thorpe in the opposite corner.

A tall, fair-haired woman, Miss Thorpe's blue gray eyes showed signs of annoyance. However, at Kate's entrance, she abandoned the hard expression and summoned a frostly smile.

"Ah, there you are at last, Kathryn." To the coachman, Julia snapped, "Don't dawdle, Smythe. We are already likely to be late."

"Yes, miss."

As the coach door slammed closed, Kate sank down upon the seat opposite Julia. "I am sorry," she said. "I should have been ready when you called. I seem to have spent too much of the morning woolgathering."

"My dear Kathryn, I perfectly understand. Quite frequently, it takes me longer to attire myself than I ever would have anticipated, but the end result is worth it. You look quite charming."

The compliment lost much of its force as Julia arched one pencil-thin brow and eyed Kate's gown in a dubious manner.

But Kate's serenity remained unruffled. She apologized to no one for the old-fashioned cut of her gowns. The pearl gray frock suited her with its low waist and soft flowing skirt, a lace-trimmed fichu draped about the shoulders, crossing modestly in the front. Her only ornament was a single red rose pinned at the valley of her breasts. Such a style was far more proper for a bishop's daughter than the latest fashions that clung so shockingly to the figure, leaving little to the imagination. It was Kate's pride that she had never had a gown from a fashionable modiste, all her clothing orders going to an impecunious widow with four children to support. By contrast, Julia's mourning garb of black silk was of the first stare of elegance, the skirt cut on severe straight lines, the matching spencer held closed by braided frogs. The ensemble was set off tastefully by a costly set of pearls and made an excellent foil for Julia's fair-haired beauty.

As the coach lurched into movement, an awkward silence settled over the interior. Kate frequently found herself not knowing what to say to Julia, which was odd, because since Kate had moved to Lytton's Dene six months ago, Miss Thorpe had proclaimed herself to be Kate's dearest friend.

Kate had never had a "dearest friend," but she had difficulty envisioning Julia in the role. Such a cool, elegant woman, nearly seven years Kate's senior, so clever it was almost alarming. Kate wondered why Julia chose to seek out such a dull companion as herself. Yet it seemed ungrateful, almost wicked to question a friendship so freely offered. Perhaps Julia was lonely, too.

But feeling as low as Kate did this morning, she would have preferred to have walked to Mapleshade, seeking a little solitude in which to compose her thoughts.

As the carriage lumbered along, Kate stared out the window to avoid Julia's penetrating gaze. The main road through Lytton's Dene passed by in a swirling haze of dust. The village was no more than a small collection of thatch-covered houses, a handful of tiny shops, and a little blue-and-white post office all set around the village green opposite the Tudor-style inn, named the Arundel Arms in honor of Harry's family.

The barouche rattled through the village in a flash. By the time they crossed the hump-backed bridge set over a trickle of stream, the spire of St. Benedict's Church came into view, and Kate became aware that Miss Thorpe was speaking of her brother.

"And Adolphus asked me to convey his apologies. He would so liked to have accompanied you. Lady Lytton expects him to deliver some sort of address at this sorry affair, extolling the virtues of my late cousin. Poor Adolphus was still scrambling to finish it when I left him.

"Rather a task." Julia essayed a laugh. "One does not like to speak ill of the dead, but it is sometimes difficult to speak good of them either."

Kate tensed as though she had received a sharp kick. "I beg your pardon?"

"Ah, I see I have shocked you. Don't misunderstand me. I was fond of Lytton. But it is difficult to eulogize a man whose best points were that he was an excellent whip and a hard rider to hounds."

"I am sure that Ha— I mean Lord Lytton had many other amiable qualities," Kate said stiffly.

"But then you did not know him very well, did you?"

Kate swallowed the urge to hotly refute that. Papa had once said nearly the same thing to her when he had feared she might be considering Harry's suit.

"Truly," Julia said, her voice filled with amusement. "What will poor Adolphus say? He can scarcely declare that Lytton was a god-fearing man."

No, Kate reluctantly had to agree. Harry had once

remarked that even drawing too near the doors of a church was likely to make him break out in hives.

"And one certainly cannot acclaim Lytton as a scholar. I doubt he ever touched a book in his life."

Yes, he had. Despite her mounting irritation, Kate bit back a smile, remembering the rainy afternoon, she had been blue-deviled, and Harry had entertained her by demonstrating what a remarkable tower could be built from her father's heavy religious tomes.

"And," the relentless Julia continued, "neither can Lytton be praised as a good landlord. One only has to glance out the window for proof of that."

She nodded toward a distant farm building they were passing, the thatched roof of which showed signs of caving in at one section. Kate recognized the structure as belonging to one of his lordship's tenants.

That she could not deny any of Julia's charges only added to Kate's misery and roused an anger within her bosom such as she rarely felt. She suppressed an impulse to snap out in Harry's defense. At least he had been unfailingly tolerant and kind, which was more than could be said of a certain sharp-tongued vicar's sister.

Kate had swallowed the remark, clenching her gloved hands in her lap, more than a little appalled by her own ill-nature. She had hailed with relief the carriage turning toward the great iron gates of the lodge that led into Mapleshade Park. Hitherto lukewarm in her feelings toward Julia, she had the notion that a moment more spent in her company and Kate would quite learn to hate her "dearest friend."

Kate had not stood more than five minutes upon the hillside when she wished she had listened to her mother. She should not have come. The sun beat down ruthlessly upon her head, yet she did not think to open her parasol. She stood gripping the ivory carved handle, standing a little apart from the others in isolated misery. A hum of bright chatter filled the air as the other ladies and gentlemen present speculated what lay beneath that mysterious mountain of canvas.

Kate realized this was not a funeral service. That had been held in the church for Harry weeks ago. This was only the dedication of his memorial, but still—! Everyone did not have to act as though this were some sort of Hyde Park fête, as though Harry had died years ago.

The only one displaying any grief was Harry's stepmama. The Dowager Lady Lytton sniffed in her black-edged handkerchief as she stood conversing with Julia. Kate, who found the old lady with her brassy curls and painted cheeks rather shocking, had been unable to do more than murmur a few polite words to her.

If such a thing had been possible, Kate thought she would far rather have stepped back a few paces and mingled with Harry's servants. From the youngest chambermaid to the stately old butler, Mr. Gravshaw, they remained somberly quiet, their faces a reflection of sorrowful respect. To Kate, there seemed to be more honest emotion in the way one of the stable lads surreptitiously wiped his eyes on his sleeve than all of Lady Lytton's elegant dabbings.

Even more did Kate wish herself far away when she drew too close to Squire Gresham and chanced to overhear some of the remarks he was making to his wife.

"You don't think it'd be considered too f'rard, do you, Sophy," he mumbled, "if I was just to drop a word in Lady Lytton's ear? There's a couple of prime hunters of Harry's I've always had my eye on and I wouldn't want anyone else stealing a march on me."

"I doubt it would do you a particle of good, Squire,"

said Mrs. Gresham. "Those horses would rightfully be the property of the new earl, his to dispose of."

"That dour cousin of Harry's from up north?" the squire growled. "A penny pinching Scot who will drive a hard bargain. Rot the luck!"

Her heart firing with indignation, Kate moved back so she did not have to hear anymore. She had scolded Harry herself for his preoccupation with his horses, but somehow the squire scheming over Harry's grave to have his favorite hunters inspired Kate with a most unchristian desire to break her parasol over Gresham's head.

It was a relief when Reverend Thorpe commanded everyone to silence and began his speech. After the first few words, Kate blotted out the sound of his voice. She did not want to her the vicar damning Harry with faint praise.

Her head thumped unpleasantly as she brushed her damp brow with the back of her glove. It was so hot. Was it only her fancy or had the breezes here been much more warm and gentle when Harry had been alive?

She could not say. She had only been to this hill-side the one time before, and that had been spring. Harry had driven her out here to ask her to be his bride. If her answer had been different, she, too, would be wearing black, but she would have had nearly two years with Harry. Nay if she had married him, perhaps he would never have gone away. She would have dissuaded him from rushing off to fight Bonaparte. Harry might still be—

Kate squeezed her eyes tight. No, she could not think such things as that. She had given Harry the only possible answer she could. Never could she have married him. If she had ever been the least unsure, matters had been made clear to her that morning Papa had called her into his study.

The bishop's silvery halo of hair had been bent

over his desk, as ever spread with pages of some scholarly text he was working upon. His stern eyes softened as he invited Kate to be seated.

He came directly to the point. Lord Lytton was being most particular in his attentions to Kate. Papa trusted that even such a reckless young man as he would not trifle with the daughter of a bishop.

"Oh, no, Papa," Kate said. Harry, after his own fashion, had ever behaved like a gentleman.

"You have developed a preference for this young man?" The bishop asked.

Kate blushed. "I—I enjoy his company." It had been a mild way to express the whirlwind effect that Harry frequently had upon her heart.

But even that admission was enough to bring a worried frown to Papa's brow, which Kate hated to see. The bishop had looked tired and ill so much of late.

Papa settled back in his chair, trying to suspend his judgment, waiting for Kate to explain what qualifications Harry possessed to make him suitable as a husband.

Kate knew her father well enough to realize he did not mean worldly possessions such as title or fortune. She stared down at the floor, embarrassed. What could she say, that Harry was like rays of sun streaking through a gray sky, that he could always make her laugh, that being with him was like waltzing through a world that was all holiday. Such fanciful considerations would not weigh with Papa, even as Kate knew she must not allow them to weigh with herself.

When she remained silent, her father began to patiently point out his own reservations. The bishop was never one to visit the sins of the father upon the child, but it was well known that old Lord Lytton, Harry's father, had been a man of great wickedness, steeped in vice. He had led his son down the same

27

path, gaming, hard drinking, indulging every wild sport while all duty had been set aside.

But Papa said nothing that Kate's own sensible mind had not already told her. Yes, indeed, Lord Harry was too irresponsible and too reckless to make a proper mate for a bishop's daughter. She and Harry were too unlike, coming from two very different worlds.

To have accepted Harry would have been to disappoint and worry her father, at a time when he was already seriously ill. She had tried to explain all that to Harry, but he would not understand. His comprehension was limited to one question. Did she love him or not?

Kate had made up her mind that she could not possibly love Harry, but she never realized what self-possession it would take to look him in the eye and tell him so.

I don't love you, my lord.

Could she have ever pronounced those words if she had not distanced herself from him by using his title? Even now Kate was not sure. Harry had not noticed her avoidance of his name. There had only been a flicker of something in his eyes. Pain? Disappointment?

He had not behaved as though his heart was broken. If anything he had been more talkative, more teasing than ever escorting her back to the carriage. It had been the last time she had ever seen him. Perhaps Harry had been relieved himself by her refusal, finally realizing how wise she had been.

Then why didn't she feel wise? Kate thought bleakly, standing here on Harry's hillside, waiting for his memorial to be unveiled, her throat burning with unshed tears.

She scarce noticed when a tall broad-shouldered man edged past her to stand behind the squire. The sound of the vicar's voice droned on as though from a great distance. Would Adolphus Thorpe never make an end? Kate swayed on her feet, only wanting this ordeal to be over before she utterly disgraced herself.

When the memorial was unveiled at last, Kate spared the statue one brief glance. A hot blush stole into her cheeks as she averted her gaze. What an outrage! What an affront to Harry's memory.

But suddenly, so clearly in her mind, she could hear the echo of Harry's teasing voice, almost feel him chucking her playfully under the chin as he had been wont to do. "Come, Kate, smile. You take things much too seriously."

The recollection was so vivid, it nearly brought the tears spilling over at last. The statue was horrid. But how Harry would have laughed. She could almost hear him. . . .

It took Kate a few seconds to realize the deep booming sound was not a product of her mind. Someone actually was laughing, roaring with it—the tall man who had brushed past her earlier.

Kate turned to gaze up at him reproachfully. She froze, encountering a pair of twinkling green eyes, the roguish smile that had haunted her dreams.

"Kate," Harry said, his smile fading.

She stared at him, her heart racing, the blood thundering in her ears. Her head swam as her eyes tried to convince her stubborn mind that the man standing before her was no chimera, no figment of her overwrought imagination.

Her lips attempted to form his name. Harry . . . Harry still alive, standing so close she had but to reach out and touch him, the answer to a prayer kept so silent, so deep within her heart, she had not even been aware of making it.

She took a faltering step toward Lord Lytton. Then, for the first time in her life, the self-possessed Miss Kathryn Towers sank down into a swoon.

Chapter 3

The world in which Kate floated was cool, dark, and soothing. She wanted to linger there as long as she could, but part of her strained toward the far-away sound of a voice calling her name.

"Kate? Kate . . . can you not hear me? Gravshaw! Hasn't anyone located those blasted smelling salts? What? Hurry, man. Hand them over."

The next instant, Kate's peace-filled darkness was disrupted by something strong and pungent being shoved beneath her nose. Moaning softly, she rolled her head to one side, trying to escape the vile odor.

"Thank God. She's coming round. Kate!" The voice came sharper, more insistent this time. Strong fingers ruthlessly chafed her wrists. "Gravshaw, go see if Sam has left to fetch the doctor. And for God's sake, keep that flock of clucking women out of here. . . ."

The voice faded as Kate fluttered her eyes open. Her first feeling was one of bewilderment. She had the vague notion that she had been napping and expected to find herself in the tiny parlor of the cottage. She blinked, her dazed eyes instead taking in the dimensions of a lofty room with tall French windows, the chamber's rich oak paneling bestrewn with paintings of the hunt. She was stretched out upon a sofa of rich brocade, a mound of cushions beneath her head.

Before she could begin to fathom where she might be, her view of the room was cut off when a tall, masculine figure loomed over her.

It was Harry. Kate had an idea that she should have been surprised to see him, yet all she felt was an unspeakable happiness at his presence.

"Kate? Are you all right?" he asked, laying his hand against her brow.

Kate experienced a childlike feeling of disappointment that his lips were not quirked in that familiar smile she so longed to see. His eyes were somber with concern, almost an element of fear lurking in them. His face had an unnatural pallor beneath his layering of tan. An absurd thought flitted through Kate's mind. He could have been a ghost.

Could have been? He *should* have been. Harry was supposed to be dead. Remembrance slapped Kate like an icy wave, dashing way the remnants of confusion as the recent scene on the hillside came back to her. Harry's monument had just been unveiled. She had heard someone laughing and turned to rebuke him only to find . . . Harry. *Alive!*

She still could not believe it. As he knelt down beside the sofa, she extended her fingers to retouch his cheek. He immediately caught her hand, encasing it in the warm strength of his own.

"Kate, darling, you will unman me if you look at me that way," he murmured. He turned his hand and pressed a kiss against her palm. "I assure you I am not some dread specter come back to haunt you."

"Harry?" she whispered. "You are alive? Truly?"

"So I have always believed, my love, but I have never been so glad of it as at this moment."

Kate choked on a joyful sob and struggled to rise, her head yet reeling.

"Nay, gently, Kate." Harry slipped one arm behind her shoulders to support her. With the other hand, he produced a tumbler of brandy that had been resting nearby on a tripod table.

But such nearness to the man she had thought dead, lost forever, was having a strange effect on Kate. Impelled by a rush of feeling such as she had never known, she startled Harry by flinging her arms about his neck, dashing the crystal glass to the floor.

Harry made a weak attempt to remonstrate, to ease her back among the cushions. He cradled her in his arms, brushing a reverent kiss upon her brow. But in the delirium of her joy, Kate quite forgot that she was a bishop's daughter. She tipped back her head, eagerly seeking his lips. Harry's eyes widened, but his noble resistance lasted no more than a second.

The warmth of Harry's lips against her own was a novel sensation to Kate. She had never kissed a man before, never daring as much even in her dreams.

She felt as though her heart stood quite still and raced madly all at the same time. She tightened her arms about him, passionately melding her mouth to his, the fire spreading more quickly through her veins than any brandy could have accomplished.

It was Harry who broke the contact, easing her away with a long, shuddering sigh.

"Damme!" He breathed, then gave a shaky laugh. "If I had any notion this was the sort of reception awaiting me, I would have despatched the French Army and come back much sooner."

A tender light came into his eyes, as he stroked a stray curl back from her brow. "But what a fright you gave me, Kate, collapsing in my arms that way."

A watery chuckle escaped Kate. What a fright she had given him! What about the way he had sprung up from nowhere after all those tormenting days when she had believed him dead? It was only now that she could acknowledge to herself exactly how much she had grieved, how much she had longed to hear the delightful peal of Harry's laughter.

Harry's laugher ... the thought somehow disturbed her glow of happiness like a pebble breaking the serene surface of a pond. Yes, Harry had been laughing, while she had been near to bursting into tears.

Kate's smile slowly faded.

Harry failed to note the change in her expression. He was trying to reconcile his memory of the prim girl who had turned down his marriage proposal with this woman who had cast herself so passionately into his arms. He did not waste too much effort in doing so. There was no surer way to destroy a miracle than to question it too closely.

If he was dreaming, he thought, leaning over Kate for another kiss, he did not want to be awakened. Too late did he see the unaccustomed flash of fire in her eyes, the blur of her hand as she struck out, soundly boxing his ears.

He had been bending over Kate in such a manner that the blow knocked him off balance and sent him sprawling back onto the carpet. Harry gaped up at the wrathful goddess who leaped to her feet, towering over him, her dark hair tumbling about her shoulders, her eyes the hue of a summer storm. If she had had any lightning bolts at her disposal, Harry sensed that he would have been done for.

"You—you heartless beast," Kate cried. "You unfeeling monster."

There was no doubt these bewildering epithets were directed at himself. She doubled up her fists as though she would fly at him again. Harry braced himself, but she merely flounced past him and took to pacing before the windows with short, furious steps, drawing in deep breaths as though trying to regain her self-control.

Harry sat up slowly, rubbing his stinging ear. He

stared at Kate in astonishment. The kiss had been startling enough, but this! Kate was the last woman in the world to offer a man violence. And what an incomprehensible shift in mood. None of this was in the least like his well-bred, even-tempered Kate. What could have possibly come over her?

Harry could think of only one explanation. He made no move to rise from the carpet, but sat dangling his hands over his knees, a beatific smile spreading over his features.

"You lied to me, Kathryn Towers," he announced triumphantly.

She paused long enough in her pacing to direct a killing glare at him. "I lied! How dare you, sir. You the most infamous liar of them all—"

"You lied to me that day on the Hill. You do love me, have done so all along."

"I do not! I quite detest you. When I think of how all this time—"

"The kiss made me a little suspicious," Harry continued unperturbed. "But the slap confirms it. You would never be so angry now if you were not head over ears in love."

Kate caught her breath in a furious hiss. She snatched up a Sevres vase from the mantle as though she would fling it at his head.

Harry grinned. "Do go ahead and throw it, Kate and I will know you completely adore me."

For one second he thought she meant to take him up on that. But with a small frustrated cry, she replaced the vase, trembling with the effort it cost her.

Harry sprang to his feet. Thinking that all would be well if he could only get her back into his arms, Harry attempted to cross the room to her. But she ducked behind a Hepplewhite chair, using the fragile piece of furniture as a barrier.

"Don't you come near me," she said, through clenched teeth.

Harry stopped, but he said in aggrieved tones, "You need not act though I was some sort of a Bluebeard. It was you who kissed me; then I got slapped for it."

"Don't you dare mention that kiss to me! You knew I was not myself. If you had been a gentleman, you would not have encouraged me."

"It would have taken more than being a gentleman," Harry retorted. "I would have had to have been dead."

"You could pretend you were," she flung back bitterly. "You seem to be remarkably good at it."

Comprehension dawned upon Harry at last as to the true source of her anger. But he was not in the least disturbed to discover that his beloved believed him capable of perpetrating such a dreadful jest. Truthfully when the devil of mischief was upon him, there were some people upon whom he would not have minded playing such a joke. But never his Kate.

That she was so enraged by her belief only afforded Harry further proof that she did care for him very deeply, more so than she was willing to admit. It was all he could do to control the ebullience of his own spirits and say to her soothingly, "Come, Kate. You are far too overexcited. Come back and sit beside me and we'll—"

She vehemently shook her head. Harry felt at an extreme disadvantage, trying to offer explanations with the chair between them,but he did not wish to upset her further. At least some of the color had come back into her cheeks.

"I did not pretend to be dead, Kate. I don't know how this infernal misunderstanding came about. I just arrived home today."

She gave a scornful sniff. "How convenient that you should have arrived just in time to attend your own dedication."

"Yes, it was convenient— I mean, it was the most dashed coincidence." Harry studied her stony profile with a sinking heart and realized she did not believe him. He could scarce blame her. "I don't pretend that in the past I might not have been capable of serving up such a trick, but never to you, Kate. Good Lord, what are you even doing here in Lytton's Dene? I had heard that after your father . . . that you had gone to live with your grandmother near Lewes."

"I moved to Lytton's Dene six months ago."

"To be closer to me?" Harry asked coaxingly.

"No! Mama admired a cottage in the village. After our period of mourning was at an end, I thought it would be good for her to still be near her old friends from Chillingsworth."

"Then why not just stay in Chillingsworth?"

When she compressed her lips together, refusing to answer, Harry smiled. "After that kiss and that slap, are you still going to deny you love me?"

"I don't intend to deny anything, because I don't ever intend to speak to you again." Kate drew herself rigidly upright. "Now if you will excuse me, my lord, I am going home."

"Kate . . ."

"What have you done with my gloves and bonnet?" She came from behind the chair to search the room in a distracted, ineffectual manner.

Harry had some vague recollection of having taken off her bonnet and flung it down upon the hillside during his first effort to rouse her from her faint. One of her gloves lay discarded by the sofa's claw leg. Harry grabbed it up.

When Kate stretched out her hand for it, he held it just out of her reach.

"Even the cruelest of ladies will let her knight have some token of remembrance," he said, hoping to wheedle a smile from her.

"A knight, certainly, but not a knave." She refused to come any closer to retrieve the article. With a stiff shrug, she said, "You may as well keep it. You appear to have lost the other one."

Turning up her heel, she stalked away. But when she reached the door, the brass knob refused to yield beneath her grasp. She rattled it, then looked accusingly at Harry.

He held up the key with an apologetic glance. "I had to do something to keep away that pack of hen-witted females. When you first fainted, Julia and the rest of 'em nigh suffocated you beneath a pile of silk fans."

"Unlock this door at once, sir."

He crossed his arms over his chest. "I don't think I shall," he said, "until you listen to what I have to say."

"You open that door right now!" She stamped her foot, then turned and tugged at the knob. "You open it or I . . . I will—"

In frustration, she struck her palm against the unmoving barrier of oak. Her shoulders sagged, and she rested her forehead against the grain, the tears beginning to trickle down her cheeks.

"Oh, lord," Harry exclaimed in horror. "No, here now, Kate. Don't do that." He rushed to her side. "I would rather face a field of bayonets all over again than make you cry."

Peering down at her, he slapped futilely at his waistcoat. He never seemed to have a damned handkerchief about him. He attempted to check the flow of crystal drops with his fingers, but she averted her face and produced her own pristine square of lace-edged linen.

Harry rested his hands on her shoulders. "Please don't cry, Kate. You know I was only teasing you. I'll unlock the blasted door at once if that's what you really want."

"I want to go home!"

"And so you shall. In my own carriage."

"No, I don't need— I came with—" But Kate appeared to think twice about what she had been about to say. Dabbing furiously at her eyes, she said with as much dignity as she could muster, "Th-thank you, my lord. I am most grateful for your offer. I should like to ride in your coach . . ."

"*Alone*," she added pointedly.

Harry sighed. How had she guessed that he fully planned on accompanying her, continuing to plead his case in the privacy of the carriage? He started to argue with her, but one glance at her tear-swollen eyes, the genuine distress marring the serenity of her features, and Harry held his tongue.

He was being a selfish brute. Kate had received a dreadful shock whether it had been of his making or not. She was clearly overwrought. Although it took all of his self-restraint, he realized the best course would be to send her home, allow her some time to compose herself. Kate was a most fair-minded woman. When she was more herself, she would be willing to listen to him. He hoped.

As she dried the last of her tears, Harry unlocked the door. When he swung the barrier open, he was considerably startled when his cousin Julia all but tumbled across the threshold.

Julia's gaze flicked from Kate's reddened eyes to Harry. His cousin subjected him to a basilisk stare. "What have you been doing to this poor girl, Lytton?"

"You ought to know," Harry said dryly. "Or did the thickness of the door prove too much for you?"

Another woman might have blushed at the implication she had been eavesdropping, but it was not so easy to discompose Julia. Ignoring Harry, she descended upon Kate.

"My dearest Kathryn, I have been so anxious about you. I would have been at your side, but between Lytton and his odious butler, I was not permitted to get near you."

Harry raised his brows in frowning surprise. When had Miss Towers become Julia's "dearest Kathryn"? He half feared that Kate would cast herself beneath Julia's protection, closing ranks in that manner women had when they feel they have been much abused by the male sex.

But Kate only murmured something indistinguishable and shrank back, showing no pleasure in Julia's solicitude. Julia rounded on Harry.

"I see that your behavior has not improved in the time you have been away, Lytton. You still have no more notion of propriety than the kitchen cat. Did it not occur to you that you could have utterly ruined Miss Tower's reputation, keeping her closeted with you in that fashion?"

As Kate blanched with dismay, Harry could have wrung his cousin's neck.

"Fortunately," Julia continued. "I had the foresight to direct the squire and his wife and all your other guests into the front salon where they are having refreshment. No one is aware of how long you and Kathryn have been alone together."

"Thank you, Julia," Harry said grimly. "It is such a relief to have you so busy upon my behalf."

She peered down the length of her nose at him. "I did not do it for you, cousin. I fear nothing will save you from the consequences of your folly this time. The latest prank of yours, appearing at your own memorial, is bound to raise such a scandal that—"

"Later, Julia," Harry broke in, observing Kate wearily touch a hand to her brow. "You can ring a peal over me as much as you please, but now I must fetch my carriage round for Kate. You can see she is still not well."

"Your carriage!" Julia said. "Kathryn came with me."

But Harry had already tucked Kate's arm beneath his own to lead her toward the curving oak stair descending into the main hall. Although Kate did not lean on him for support, neither did she attempt to pull away. Harry had the feeling that she was as relieved as he was to be escaping Julia's clacking tongue.

But Miss Thorpe was not so easily vanquished. She trailed after them, insisting she would take Kathryn home. Harry, however, had had long experience in fobbing off Julia's attempts to order him about, and he prevented her from riding roughshod over Kate as well since she seemed in no state to defend herself.

By the time Harry led her out to the gravel drive circling Mapleshade's front lawn, Kate looked exhausted from Julia's badgering. He handed her into the recesses of his most comfortable and well-sprung coach. At the last second, one of the gardeners came rushing up with Kate's bonnet.

Leaning in through the carriage's open door, Harry passed it up to her, the garment much the worse from his previous rough handling of it, the poke front crushed beyond redemption.

Kate took the bonnet from him without a word.

"I shall come to call upon you soon, Kate," he said.

Kate stared stonily straight in front of her. "I fear I shall not be at home, my lord."

"What! At two in the morning?"

This sally did not produce so much as the quiver of a response. Harry sighed. He hated letting her go this way. Swallowed up in the vastness of the coach, she looked so small, so prim and obstinate, so completely adorable, he longed for nothing more than to gather her up in his arms.

"I don't suppose this is a good moment to ask you again to marry me?" he said wistfully. At her reproachful glare, he threw up one hand in a peace-making gesture. "One cannot hang a man for asking, Kate."

Making her his best leg, he closed the door and stepped back, giving the coachman the signal to whip up the horses.

"And now that I am convinced you love me," Harry muttered. "I *will* ask you, Kate. Again and again, until one of these days you are going to forget yourself and say yes."

Shading his eyes, he followed the coach's progress down the long drive until it disappeared into the line of trees fronting the park. Sighing, Harry turned back toward the house. Despite the unsatisfactory nature of his reunion with Kate, he moved with a lighthearted spring to his step, feeling far different from the man, who only a matter of a few hours ago, had trudged past his empty fields.

Hope was a heady draught, and Harry felt nigh drunk with it. With his hands on his hips, he paused to stare up at his home, feeling somehow that he had never fully appreciated the old hall. At one time a medieval manor house, two projecting wings had been added after the Restoration, along with hipped roofs and a balustrade. But the original brickwork, although now considered unfashionable, remained untouched, and Harry vowed that it would continue to be so during his lifetime. It gave the hall a much warmer glow than those modern facing tiles of silvery white.

Imagining the day when he would bring Kate across the threshold as his bride, Harry doted upon every brick of the old place. He doted upon the huge stone lions that stood guarding the forecourt, upon the unspoiled expanse of lawn.

But his present rush of good humor did not quite extend to doting upon the tall fair-haired man who awaited him in the manor's open doorway.

Although not fond of Reverend Thorpe, Harry did

not dislike his cousin either. At times he even thought Adolphus was not a bad sort, except when he appeared to be half-choking on his clerical collar.

As Harry strode up the steps to join the vicar beneath the portico, he noted with half-humorous dismay the way Reverend Thorpe tugged at his starched neckband as though to draw attention to the badge of his authority.

"Cousin Harry," he said sternly.

"Cousin Adolphus," Harry replied pleasantly.

"My lord, I scarce know what to say to you—"

Being familiar with Adolphus, Harry was damned sure he was going to think of something. "Whatever it is, I am sure it can keep till later. I am done in. It has been, saving your presence, one hell of a day."

"Others might say the same. You should go to your stepmother at once and beg her pardon for the distress you have brought her. She is prostrate, my lord, completely prostrate."

"A man is only entitled to have one female swoon in his arms per day, Adolphus. I have already had mine. You may feel quite free to take on the next one."

"My lord!" the vicar explained in outraged accents.

"Believe me, Adolphus," Harry said. "I am not being totally unfeeling. For me to go to Sybil would be like exposing an already sick woman to a case of the pox. She will be much more ready to receive me when she has recovered a little."

Harry managed to edge past the vicar, slipping inside the hall, only to run dead into Julia. He was not surprised this time. Julia was frequently to be found hovering at her brother's elbow.

She glowered at Harry, apparently still annoyed with him for having whisked Kate out of her clutches.

"Lytton, I must speak to you. Your conduct—"

Harry stopped her with an upraised hand. "My

dear Julia, I know I promised you the pleasure of giving me a setdown, but I fear it must once again be deferred. I must have a word with all those guests you so obligingly herded into the front salon, perhaps even raise a glass with the squire. Timothy Keegan informs me that English memorial services are sadly wanting, and I feel I should do something to raise our reputation."

Having effectively rendered both of the Thorpes speechless with indignation, Harry strolled on his way, whistling cheerfully.

Although the gathering in the salon never reached the proportions of what Keegan would have termed a passable wake, the atmosphere became much more convivial with Harry's entrance. The ladies fussed over him and called him a naughty rogue; the squire swearing that by gawd, even if his lordship did keep refusing to sell those hunters, the squire was damned glad to see the lad home safe again.

The only ones of the party to leave early were the Thorpes. The vicar's barouche rumbled down the drive at a great speed as though eager to distance itself from the hall and the return of its incorrigible master.

Julia stared out the coach window, her flawless profile as hard and unyielding as if carved of marble. She bore the dubious distinction of being acclaimed the loveliest spinster in the shire. Her beauty had never been enough to compensate for her lack of fortune or her fixed belief that she could improve the character of any man she met.

She even felt that she could have redeemed her cousin Harry if he had ever asked her to be his wife. But as his lordship had never shown the good sense to make her an offer, Julia had long ago washed her hands of him. She was not so ill-natured as to wish that Lord Lytton *had* died at Waterloo, but his return promised to be a great nuisance, especially from what Julia had already observed of his attentions toward Kate.

It was not that Julia was in the least jealous on her own account. No, the chief source of her vexation was that she had already marked Miss Kathryn Towers down for her own brother.

As the carriage rattled past the park gates, Julia turned to the vicar seated opposite her and broke the rigid silence they had maintained since leaving the hall.

"Well! Now that Lytton has returned, you may be assured, he will be stirring up some mischief."

"There is nothing new in that, my dear," Adolphus said wearily.

"I fear he may have already begun . . . with Kathryn Towers." Julia observed her brother closely for his reaction.

Adolphus's eyes widened. "Why, I thought that was one of Lord Harry's more commendable actions today, his solicitude for Miss Towers."

Solicitude! Julia pressed her hand to her eyes, the degree of her brother's naïveté as ever confounding her. Only a blind man would have mistaken the lover-like way Lytton had swooped up Kathryn in his arms and charged back to the house with her as being mere solicitude. His lordship had appeared suitably distraught and heroic enough to set several more young ladies off into a swoon.

"Lytton's attentions to Kathryn were most improper," Julia said. "As her friend he should have allowed me to take care of her. He actually thrust me aside. I could not hear all that he said to her when they were alone in the Hunt parlor but—"

"Julia! You were never eavesdropping."

"It was my moral obligation to do so. Lytton was practically holding the poor girl a prisoner in that room."

"I cannot believe that even Lytton would seek to molest a respectable young woman beneath the roof of his ancestral home."

"He was not molesting her. I think he is trying to fix his interest with her."

"What! On such brief acquaintance?"

"He had met her before," Julia explained with strained patience. "Two years ago in Chillingsworth. There were even rumors that Lytton wished to marry Kathryn, but the bishop would have none of it."

"Oh." Adolphus blinked.

Julia found the single syllable as a reply most unsatisfactory.

"Is that all you have to say?" she demanded, "when I have just told you that your ne'er-do-well cousin may be planning to steal your intended bride."

Adolphus's lips curved in a deprecating smile. "I would scarce dare call Miss Towers so. We are not on such terms as that."

"You could be, if you would make the slightest push. Have I not told you that she is perfect for you, Adolphus? Absolutely perfect?

"Yes, you have, my dear. Upon many occasions." Adolphus squirmed. "Miss Towers is a most amiable young woman, but—"

"Amiable! She is modest, well-favored, bred to be a clergyman's wife and . . . and simply perfect," Julia finished by breaking off what she had actually been about to say. It would do no good to point out to one as lacking in ambition as Adolphus Kathryn's other charms. Although only possessed of a respectable competence, Kathryn's chief fortune lay in her connections. She had one uncle highly placed in the cabinet of the present ministry, to say nothing of her circle of acquaintances within the cathedral close at Chillingsworth. It was most unfortunate that her father, the bishop, should be dead, but Kate still retained enough influential friends to be certain that her future husband would not be left to languish as parson of some obscure country vicarage. Julia intended to see her brother become a dean or at least an archdeacon with several livings at his disposal.

Adolphus should see for himself what a good match Kathryn would be, but instead his handsome brow furrowed into a troubled frown.

"You may be right, Julia— I mean, of course you are right," he hastily amended. "Miss Towers is perfect, but if, as you believe, Lord Harry should have some notion of settling down and wish to wed the young lady, I do not feel it would be right to set myself up as rival to him."

As Julia fixed him with a cold stare, her brother stammered, "Y-you tend to forget my position here. Although he is our cousin, Harry is also lord of the manor. I can never provoke his lordship while I owe him such a debt of gratitude. It was he who presented me with the living—"

"Lytton would have presented St. Benedict's to the first tinker coming down the lane," Julia said scornfully, "if only to spare himself further responsibility in the matter."

Thus dismissing her brother's obligations to Lord Lytton, Julia proceeded to inform Adolphus how he should call upon Kathryn at once to see how she fared, perhaps even take her a small nosegay from the parsonage garden. But neither coaxing or insisting could move him to do so.

"I have a sermon to finish for the morrow," Adolphus said, his jaw cutting in stubborn fashion.

Julia saw that nothing she could say would convince him and, although considerably annoyed, was obliged to give over for the moment. Adolphus could be led to a certain point, but when he waxed obstinate, it was best to let be or she would only have more difficulty reopening the subject of his courtship later.

Julia had realized a long time ago that she was much more clever than her younger brother. She would never have been so unmaidenly as to admit being discontent with her lot, a frustration that her sex barred her from the education that seemed to have been wasted upon Adolphus. Instead, she found her solace by managing his life for him.

It distressed her when she thought that perhaps Adolphus might truly be content to be no more than the vicar of Lytton's Dene. She had far greater plans for him, and neither his modesty nor Lytton's interference were going to ruin these schemes.

When they arrived at the vicarage, Adolphus's last word on the subject was to pat her kindly on the shoulder and tell her not to fret. "I am sure the Almighty will decide whom your good friend Kathryn should marry."

Although Julia bowed her head in pious acquiescence, she realized that the Almighty frequently had a way of arranging things not to her satisfaction. But not this time, she thought, her lips thinning dangerously. Not if she had anything to say in the matter.

Come what may, Julia vowed, Lord Lytton would not have Kate.

Chapter 4

Maisie Towers settled herself upon the window seat and stole one glance through the sun-glazed panes, hoping for some sign of a carriage billowing in a dusty cloud along the lane. Surely Kate should have been home by now, Mrs. Towers began to fret, then adjured herself not to be a fool. Kate was not likely to break any bones attending a dedication service upon a hillside.

No, not any bones, Mrs. Towers thought, suppressing a worried sigh, *only a heart.* She forced her gaze away from the window and summoned an attentive smile for her guests, all the while wishing them at Jericho.

Mrs. Prangle, the archdeacon's wife, had been ensconced upon the settee for over half an hour, her inquisitive eyes taking in every detail of the cottage, her sharp, unlovely voice rasping at Mrs. Towers's nerves. Seated upon either side of Mrs. Prangle were her two red-haired daughters. Doubtless in a few years they would grow to be most sensible girls, but now they showed a distressing tendency to giggle.

"And I told archdeacon," Mrs. Pringle trilled on, "that I was going out this way to visit my sister in any case, so I must stop and call upon Maisie Towers and dear Kathryn. Such as pity she should be away from home."

Mrs. Towers smiled, nodded, and wished she had accompanied her daughter.

Mrs. Prangle arched her neck, glancing about her. "This is a charming house, although rather small. Have you got but the one parlor? And such a tiny dining room. Rather a change for you, my dear, after the splendor of the bishop's palace."

The Misses Prangle giggled their agreement.

"The cottage is large enough for Kate and me," Mrs. Towers said mildly. She liked the coziness of her small house, although at the moment she wished it were located at the tip of Wales, too far for Mrs. Prangle and the other gossipy ladies of Chillingsworth to call. Dear Kate had meant to be so kind, arranging it that her mother should be near her old acquaintances. Mrs. Towers had been quite unable to tell the poor child she had no desire to see most of those prying women again.

"The late bishop, rest his soul, was such a saintly man," Mrs. Prangle said, her bonnet feathers nodding as she mounted a fresh attack. "He never used his position to amass a fortune as some might have done, did he?"

This was such a bald-faced attempt to discover how Mrs. Towers and Kate had been left circumstanced, that Mrs. Towers stiffened. She had never known how to depress such impertinence. Kate would have known how to answer Mrs. Prangle. Kate had always known, far better than her retiring mother, how to deal with the never-ending stream of canons' wives, prebendaries' daughters and vicars' nieces who had trickled through the drawing rooms of the bishop's palace.

But Kate was not here, and Mrs. Towers did the best she could. She succeeded in changing the subject by inquiring after the archdeacon's son at Eton.

As Mrs. Prangle boasted how young George had become the boon companion of a duke's son, the china clock upon the mantel chimed three. Mrs. Towers noted with alarm that Mrs. Prangle might linger until tea time and that Kate still had not returned home.

Her anxious gaze traveled to the window once more. She had never been able to divine the true extent of Kate's feelings for the late Lord Lytton, but all her motherly instincts told her that her daughter was hiding a great deal of pain.

She should have put her foot down, duty be hanged, and not permitted Kate to go through the ordeal of attending that dedication. But she never had been able to take a firm line with Kate. Sometimes she stood a little in awe of her own daughter, so reserved, so self-possessed, so much like her father—

"Ooh!"

Mrs. Towers was startled from her thoughts by a squeal of delight from the youngest Miss Prangle. "Can that be Miss Towers coming home now? What an elegant coach!"

Mrs. Towers had allowed her mind to wander so far, that she had been unaware that a conveyance had pulled her up before the gate, but not the one she looked for. Before she could obtain a clearer view, the other three women joined her at the window, and she was nigh suffocated by a profusion of bouncing curls and muslin gowns.

Managing to peer past Mrs. Prangle's feathers, Mrs. Towers determined that it was not the vicar's smart barouche, but a much more impressive coach, fit to have been a state carriage for royalty.

"Look at the coat of arms on the door," Miss Prangle exclaimed. "Would that be the Arundel family crest?"

"No," Mrs. Towers said, a chill of recognition

coursing through her. "It-it is . . ." The Prangles regarded her breathlessly. "It is . . . my mother-in-law," Mrs. Towers said.

The sight of the grande dame being handed from the coach by a bewigged footman in scarlet and gold livery caused the Prangles to shiver with excitement but Mrs. Towers's heart sank in dismay.

Winifred Aldarcie Towers, the Lady Dane, had been widowed for many years now. One of her chief forms of amusement was to descend unexpectedly upon the families of her numerous offspring. With the bishop in his grave, Mrs. Towers had considered herself safe from any more such visitations. How disconcerting to discover she was wrong.

As Mrs. Prangle and her tittering daughters fussed, smoothing out their gowns and hair, Mrs. Towers rose to her feet with all the resignation of a condemned prisoner.

All too soon the door to the parlor opened, the pert Mollie entering the room in subdued fashion.

"Lady Dane," Mollie announced in awed accents.

She flattened herself against the door as her ladyship swept past. Lady Dane stalked into the parlor with all the majesty of a queen, leaning upon a silver-handled cane she in nowise needed, her bearing still upright, her step unhampered despite her advancing years. Her figure had lost none of its statuesque proportions, her eye none of its keenness. The only signs of age were the lovely waves of white hair flowing back from her brow, the feathering of lines upon her skin, which only seemed to draw attention to the aristocratic fineness of her bone structure.

Even in her youth something in Winifred Towers's countenance had made all the young men tremble in her presence, address her as madam. Only one had ever been privileged to see the softness of her smiles and that had been the bandy-legged little Baron of Dane whom she had chosen to marry.

No hint of that smile now transformed Lady Dane's features as she crossed the threshold of the tiny parlor, her hawklike gaze taking in both the chamber and its occupants. Mrs. Towers forced herself forward to greet her ladyship.

"Mother Towers. What a surprise."

"Maisie." Lady Dane unbent enough to offer her cheek, which Mrs. Towers dutifully saluted. She had then no choice but to present Mrs. Prangle and her daughters, who embarked upon a frenzied round of curtsying.

After subjecting the Prangles to a glacial stare, Lady Dane condescended to extend two fingers by way of greeting.

"I had the privilege of meeting your ladyship before at Chillingsworth," Mrs. Prangle gushed, "though I daresay my lady has forgotten."

"I daresay that I have," Lady Dane said. Her ladyship had a most royally impressive habit of rolling her *r*'s.

As abashed as Mrs. Prangle appeared, she was fully prepared to renew the acquaintance and made a movement to herd her daughters back to the settee.

"You must not think of staying upon my account," Lady Dane said in arctic accents. "I fear Maisie has already kept you beyond the time considered civil for an afternoon call."

Mrs. Prangle flushed a bright red but for once appeared unable to find anything to say. With scarce more than the raising of an eyebrow, Lady Dane sent the archdeacon's wife and daughters bustling toward the door.

This high-handed maneuver almost put Mrs. Towers in charity with her ladyship. Returning from seeing the Prangles to their coach, a gentle laugh escaped her as she asked Lady Dane, "However did you guess that woman had outstayed her welcome?"

"It required no great perspicacity. A most vulgar female," her ladyship pronounced. "*I* should have told my maid to deny that I was at home."

Mrs. Towers felt certain that her ladyship would, but she was not made of such stern stuff. Despite Lady Dane's masterly disposal of the Prangles, Mrs. Towers's smile vanished when she saw the footman dragging into the hall several large trunks to say nothing of a dressing case, her ladyship's maid following, her arms full of a supply of her ladyship's own bed linens. "I trust you have a chamber available for me?" Lady Dane asked. "Yes, of course," Mrs. Towers said, considerably dismayed by this invasion. She retained presence of mind to direct the footman and lady's maid upstairs to the proper bedchamber before inviting Lady Dane to be seated in the parlor.

"I shall have Mollie bring in some tea."

"I prefer lemonade," said her ladyship.

Mrs. Towers did not believe they had lemons in the kitchen, but she knew her small household held Lady Dane in such awe that her housekeeper would procure some forthwith.

Having given her instructions, by the time Mrs. Towers returned to the parlor, she discovered that Lady Dane had eschewed the settee vacated by the Prangles and had enthroned herself upon a stiff-backed chair.

Seating herself upon the settee, Mrs. Towers nervously inquired after her ladyship's health. She had heard that Lady Dane had gone to take the waters in Bath. Had her ladyship just returned from there?

Lady Dane returned a brief answer. Never one to engage in idle chatter, she demanded abruptly, "Where is Kathryn?"

"She is gone to attend the dedication of poor Lord Lytton's memorial. I expect her home at anytime."

Her ladyship offered no comment, merely scowling at the information. "I saw Kathryn briefly in London a fortnight ago. Did she tell you?"

"She mentioned it." Mrs. Towers had encouraged Kate to visit her cousin in the hopes that a little varied society might improve her spirits. "Kate only stayed a week. I suppose summer is not the best time to be in the city."

"The child looked positively haggard," Lady Dane said.

"She had been ill with a severe bout of influenza."

"Stuff! She is pining away for that young man, Lord Harry."

"I fear you are mistaken, my lady," Mrs. Towers said quietly. "Kate insists she did not love him."

Lady Dane gave her that look that always made Mrs. Towers feel like a perfect widgeon.

"Humpfh! The girl might be able to throw dust in your eyes, Maisie, but—"

Her ladyship broke off at the sound of another carriage arriving. Mrs. Towers glanced toward the window and saw her daughter alighting and coming up the walk at last. She thought she would have done anything to spare Kate her ladyship's overwhelming presence at this moment. She wished that Lady Dane would be kind enough not to mention Lord Harry, but one could scarce tell her ladyship to mind her tongue. Mrs. Towers took a hesitant step forward, thinking that at least she might warn Kate of her grandmother's arrival.

But it was already too late, for the parlor door came flying open. Mrs. Towers was not prepared for the flushed young woman who bolted into the chamber, her bonnet missing, her eyes sparkling with indignation.

"Mama, you will never guess what—" Kate stopped in midsentence at the sight of Lady Dane. "Grandmother!" Kate's greeting betokened surprise and a hint of wariness.

She recovered enough to kiss her ladyship's up-turned cheek in the approved manner. Kate cast a doubtful glance toward her mother as though seeking an explanation for Lady Dane's presence. Miss Towers could only respond by a bewildered shake of her head.

Lady Dane rapped her cane upon the carpet. "Don't keep us in suspense, miss. I gather something untoward happened at the dedication? Likely Sybil Arundel made a spectacle of herself as usual."

Lady Dane's remark snapped Kate's attention back to the original source of her agitation. She remained silent a moment, then burst out, "It has nothing to do with Lady Lytton. It's Lord Harry. He's still alive."

"What!" Mrs. Towers exclaimed in the same breath as Lady Dane.

"He arrived at his own dedication," Kate cried. "He had just been pretending to be dead all this time."

Mrs. Towers was as shocked and aggrieved by such conduct as her daughter, but Lady Dane broke into one of her rare trills of laughter.

"The rogue! I wish I had been there to see it. He must have made you all look like a parcel of fools, standing about in this blazing heat to gape at some ridiculous memorial."

"I didn't find it so amusing, Grandmama," Kate said in a taut voice.

"Of course. *You* wouldn't." Although still chuckling, her ladyship's eyes held a gleam of sympathy. " 'Tis most understandable you should be somewhat distressed, considering you are not exactly indifferent to the young man."

Somewhat distressed! This seemed such a callous way of describing Kate's distraught state that Mrs. Towers cast a reproachful glance at her mother-in-law. She moved closer to Kate, intending to slip a comforting arm about her daughter's waist, but Kate scarce seemed to notice the gesture.

"I *was* indifferent to Lord Lytton before, Grandmama," Kate said drawing herself up proudly, "but now I quite despise the man. If you will excuse me, I must go and change before tea."

"Kate!" But Mrs. Towers's gentle protest was lost as Kate dashed out of the room. She longed to go after her daughter, but past experience had taught her it would do little good. Sagging down upon the settee, her head spun with the shock of the tidings. Lord Lytton still alive . . .

Only Lady Dane appeared quite unperturbed.

"I told you the girl was in love with him."

Kate fled upstairs. She had been longing for the sanctuary of her own room ever since her flustered exit from Mapleshade Hall and Harry's disturbing presence. Stepping inside the small bedchamber, Kate closed the door behind her and leaned upon against it with a tremulous sigh.

The room's walls were painted green, a soothing shade that captured the softer hues of the forest. The only furnishings were the four-poster bed, the wardrobe, a washstand, a dressing table, and a chair, all carved of satinwood, all of the utmost simplicity appropriate to a clergyman's daughter, except for a few touches of lace here and there that her feminine heart *would* crave.

Yet for once the room's sylvan peacefulness was little balm to Kate's troubled spirits. She stalked away from the door, trying to draw rein upon her emotions, flattering herself that in some measure she had begun to do so.

The delusion lasted until she got a glimpse of herself in the mirror affixed to the dressing table. She all but shrank from the bonnetless hoyden staring back at her, a hectic flush coloring her face, her dark curls in a tangle. Kate pressed her hands to her cheeks in dismay. She looked like a wild woman, and to think that she had appeared thus before Lady Dane of all people. Kate had the feeling her grandmother did not approve of her in any case—a most novel and disturbing sensation to one accustomed to always meeting with approbation.

Lowering herself onto the chair, Kate started to snatch up a pearl-handled brush, then froze. Leaning closer to the mirror, her eyes widened in horror. Her mouth! She touched one trembling fingertip to lips that to her mind appeared swollen and bruised. She groaned. All the world must guess how she had been kissing Harry Arundel.

Kate's gaze strayed to the miniature of her father upon the dressing table, the bishop's stern eyes regarding her from the silver frame. With a guilty start, Kate laid the portrait face down.

Bad enough that she had embraced Harry in such wanton fashion, but she had actually struck him in a fit of temper like some brawling tavern wench. She had had every provocation to do so, but it was not the icily bred reaction to be expected of a lady, let alone the propriety demanded of a bishop's daughter.

Utterly sunk in her own esteem, Kate rested her arms upon the dressing table. Laying her head down, she finally gave vent to the stormy bout of tears that had been brewing for hours. She cried like an overtired child who had too many events crammed in one day, weeping out her shame over her own conduct.

It was some time before her sobs ceased. When she at last raised her head, she felt drained but somehow the better for it. She trudged over to the washstand and poured water from the pitcher into the basin. Splashing the cold liquid over her face, she cleansed away the ravages of her tears.

Drawing in a steadying breath, she straightened,

feeling more able to face the future . . . a future that now had to include Harry very much alive, who had come crashing back into her life once more. Whatever was she going to do?

For a moment, she harbored a cowardly wish to be far from Lytton's Dene. It would not be easy to confront Harry again, especially knowing his feelings toward her remained the same. He still wanted her. As gratifying as that was, she could no more accept Harry now than two years ago. If anything the case was more impossible now that the bishop was dead. It would be as though she had waited until poor Papa was in his grave to seek out the man he would not have wished her to marry.

This mad prank of Harry's, pretending to be dead, only served to reinforce Kate's own doubts about him. She required a more serious turn of mind in the man she would deem suitable as a husband. No, she was as resolved as ever. She and Harry would not suit.

Yet in making this resolution, Kate new she was not reckoning with one powerful force. Harry, himself. That wretched kiss! Whatever had possessed her? She had just been coming out of a swoon. She hadn't in the least known what she was doing, but she would never be able to convince Harry of that. Never would he give her any peace.

She could refuse to see him as she had threatened, but she knew Harry far too well. He would not be turned away by a tale of her not being at home. He was perfectly capable of coming round at two in the morning and chucking pebbles at her window.

She would have to see him again, but where would she find the composure to do so? Seeking strength, she turned to the one source she had been taught to trust since a child.

Dropping to her knees by the bed, she folded her

hands and raised her eyes earnestly to the chamber's scrolled ceiling.

"Dear Father in Heaven," she prayed, "give me the wisdom to deal with Harry. Help me to keep him at arm's length."

But even God did not seem to be heeding Kate today. Instead of any comforting feeling of assurance, she was visited by an image of Harry so strong her breath snagged in her throat. Not the Harry of the wicked grin, but the way he looked those sweet, rare times, his eye darkening in that fashion that made her heart pound harder, his lips curving so tenderly.

Kate sighed. Somehow her prayer for deliverance turned into a grateful flow of thanksgiving at finding Harry so very much alive.

And that prayer, she had the strangest notion, God had heard.

Kate's own resolves about Lord Harry notwithstanding, her future conduct to the earl of Lytton was already being decided upon by her formidable grandmother.

From her throne in the parlor, Lady Dane sipped her lemonade and informed Mrs. Towers, "This entirely changes everything. The purpose of my visit here was to persuade you to allow me to take Kate abroad, try to restore some life back into the girl. With the young man dead, this is the worst place she could be, but with Lytton alive . . . ah, that is entirely another matter. She must stay put until the marriage is all arranged."

Mrs. Towers thought her mother-in-law was marching a deal too fast. "But you heard what Kate said—"

"I heard." Her ladyship's mouth hooked into a fleeting smile.

"Even before Lord Lytton's outrageous prank," Mrs. Towers said, "Kate would not have thought of marrying him. The bishop never approved of him."

"That doesn't surprise me," her ladyship sniffed. She stared up at the three-quarter length portrait of her son mounted above the mantel. A most handsome man garbed in the full glory of the robes of his divine calling, it should have been a sight calculated to bring pride to any mother's heart. That it did not find great favor with Lady Dane scarcely surprised Mrs. Towers. Her late husband and his mother had never dealt well together. It was something she had never understood—how without shouting, never once raising their well-modulated voices, the pair of them could make the tension in a room thicker than the puddings served with the Sunday beef. Even with her son dead, Lady Dane made no odds about her feelings.

"Dylan was never my favorite child. Too stiffnecked by half. I always feared that Kate was cut from the same cloth. But when I saw her with Lord Harry that last winter, the girl had become almost human. I should have taken a hand in the matter then. But I am determined to rectify my negligence now. Kate is going to marry the Earl of Lytton."

Mrs. Towers heard this pronouncement with dismay, fearing her ladyship's interference was only bound to make the situation worse. Although she knew trying to turn Lady Dane aside from her determined course would be like attempting to stop a tidal wave, Mrs. Towers made one last desperate appeal.

"I fear it won't do, my lady. In many ways, Kate is like her papa. She is a most serious-minded girl. Charming as Lord Lytton is, I fear he will never be respectable enough for her.

"He shall be made respectable enough," Lady Dane announced. "I shall see to it."

Mrs. Towers was hard pressed to stifle a groan. Her heart filled with dread, foreseeing that the peace of their days at Lytton Dene were quite coming to an end. Much as she, too, wished to see Kate happily wed, she felt a pang of sympathy for Lord Lytton, who could have no notion of the storm about to descend upon him. Mrs. Towers had a strong desire to despatch a note of warning to that unfortunate young man.

Chapter 5

The master bedchamber at Mapleshade Hall stretched out with the vastness of a ballroom, the walls hung with sixteenth century Flemish tapestries, the massive fireplace carved of white marble. The chamber had originally been designed by the first Earl of Lytton for the entertainment of his king, the monogram of Charles Stuart still to be found upon the elaborately carved ceiling.

After the death of the Merry Monarch and the succession of dour James, royalty ceased to visit Mapleshade, and the next generation of Arundels gradually appropriated the magnificent chamber for their own use.

To the present earl, tucked away behind the heavy gold damask bedcurtains, the chamber spoke not of any glorious past or imposing grandeur. Lord Harry was conscious only of how good it felt to be back in his own bed.

As fatigued as he had been, the night passed in a deep sleep of oblivion. Only as the hours of morning began to sift by, did dreamings overtake him.

"Kate," he murmured, caught in that pleasing semistate between dozing and waking. Nestling his face deeper among the pillows, he imagined her removing her bonnet, shaking loose her fall of dusky curls, the tresses tumbling all silken over his fingers. Her eyes were shy and inviting, her mouth warm and eager.

He heaved a contented sight at the vision he had conjured. Somehow he had always known that beneath the prim facade of the bishop's daughter beat the heart of a most passionate woman. With a muzzy smile, he clutched at his pillow, recalling the sensation of Kate in his arms, all soft and yielding.

His fantasy was rudely disrupted by a sharp rap upon the bedchamber door. Harry ignored the brisk summons. It had to be a mistake. His servants knew better than to disturb him at this hour of a Sunday.

He tried to drift back into his dream, concentrating on the carnelian outline of Kate's lips. But his imagined kiss was again interrupted by a second knock, louder than the first. Harry responded with a snarl.

The fool in the hall beyond must have taken it for encouragement to enter. Harry heard the door creaking open.

"My lord?"

"He's not here," Harry mumbled, then cursed at the football on the carpet. Someone drew open the bedcurtains a crack, allowing a sliver of light to fall across his face. "What the devil—"

Harry focused on the upright form of this butler. Gravshaw's face was screwed up into the most peculiar expression. It took Harry a full minute to realize that the impassive manservant was actually in a state of some agitation.

Harry regarded him through bleary eyes. "Whatever has happened, this time I am not responsible."

"Oh, my Lord. There—there is this woman belowstairs."

"Miss Towers?" Harry shot up onto one elbow, the absurd hope stirring him more fully awake.

"No, my lord. She says she—"

"Then send the wench packing," Harry said, losing interest. He rolled over, drawing the coverlet up to his ears, adding with a yawn, "In the future send away all applicants for my hand. Tell them the post has been filled."

"My lord!" Gravshaw persisted, "It is an elderly female. She says—"

"She must be here to see Sybil. Direct her to my stepmother and leave me in peace."

Harry put an end to the conversation by stuffing his head under the pillow. As though from a great distance, he heard Gravshaw's despairing, "Very good, my lord," and then the muffled sound of the door closing again.

Harry emerged from beneath the pillow, believing he had heard the last of the incident. He had just succeeded in recapturing his drowsy state, embarking upon another delicious dream of Kate, when the chamber door slammed open again, this time accompanied by the sound of bickering voices, the stentorian tones of his butler and the militant accent of some unknown female.

"Madam, I beg you. His lordship does not receive callers—"

"Stand out of my way, you gibbering fool."

"My lady, this is most unseemly."

"Idiot. I am old enough to be his grandmother."

"But my lady," Gravshaw implored. "Think of your own reputation."

"At my time of life," came the tart reply, "if there be any who think scandal of my being in a young man's bedchamber, the more fool they."

Harry had the feeling that Gravshaw was getting the worst of this exchange, a notion that was reinforced when he detected the rustle of skirts advancing upon the bed. The next Harry knew his bedcurtains were wrenched open. He winced at the sudden flaring of light.

"Madam!" He heard Gravshaw huff.

Harry struggled to a sitting position, flinging one hand across his eyes. "Gravshaw. What the deuce!"

"My lord. I tried to keep her out," Gravshaw moaned. "But it was impossible short of offering her ladyship bodily harm."

"It would have been worse for you, my man, if you had tried it." The apparition standing over Harry's bed pounded a cane against the floor. Harry's dazed eyes took in the figure of a most regal lady with a countenance stern enough to have daunted the entire French line.

"Off with you, sirrah," this strange woman commanded Gravshaw. "Fetch Lord Lytton his breakfast."

Gravshaw glanced at Harry, clearly appealing for his intervention. Harry shoved back the strands of hair tumbling into his eyes, trying to convince himself that he was awake and not strayed into the midst of some mad nightmare.

"Begging your pardon, madam," he said, "but I think you must be in the wrong house. I don't believe I have had the pleasure—"

"I am Lady Dane," the woman ripped out.

Harry, who slept in the state nature intended, dragged the counterpane higher across the dark hairs matting his bared chest. "I trust your ladyship will forgive me if I don't make you my leg, but—"

"Impertinent rogue! I am Kathryn's grandmother."

Harry's jaw dropped open. Kate's grandma? Oh, Lord! The reason for this rather unorthodox morning call seemed to become abundantly clear to him. His gaze skated uneasily to the rigid form of his butler.

"Perhaps you *had* better go, Gravshaw."

"Very good, my lord," Gravshaw said at his most wooden. It was his pride that he had never permitted

65

any unbidden guests to enter the house, let alone the master's bedchamber. With a somewhat crestfallen air, he retired from the field.

Harry's attention swept back to the woman who had bested his indomitable butler. Lady Dane's stance was unyielding as iron, and Harry took to the defensive.

"I don't know all that Kate might have told you about yesterday. I expect you have every right to be angry with me, but I don't intend to apologize for that kiss. It was the first time I have ever been that bold with Kate and—"

"Hold a moment, sir." The first hinting of amusement crossed Lady Dane's stern features. "You don't know Kate very well if you imagine she came talebearing to me. The girl didn't get all that color in her face just from the sun. But if you think that I am here to scold you, my Lord, you are far off the mark."

"Then why are you here?" Harry asked.

"I shall tell you when you are more suitably attired to receive a lady."

Turning away from him, she stalked down the length of the room, flinging back over her shoulder, "And don't dawdle."

Harry stared after her a moment in a dumbfounded silence. But curiosity soon roused him to action. Obviously Lady Dane hadn't come to rip up at him over some fancied insult toward Kate. So what did she want of him?

Pushing the bed covers aside, Harry scrambled for the door that led to the adjoining dressing room. He shrugged into a pair of breeches and white shirt, then donned a satin dressing gown, belting it with a sash. Pausing to peek in the mirror, he ran his hand thoughtfully over his jaw, but he sensed that her ladyship was not the sort to take offense at the sight of an unshaven male. She was more likely to be annoyed if he kept her waiting. Swiftly combing his hair, he dashed some water on his face and returned to the bedchamber.

Gravshaw had just entered, bearing the tray with the breakfast Lady Dane had ordered for Harry. She directed the butler to place it upon a table before the empty fireplace, the hearth swept clean for the summer. Gravshaw was then dismissed. He exited from the room, the picture of affronted dignity.

Harry watched as Lady Dane settled herself into the depths of a wing-back chair and proceeded to pour out the coffee. His lips twitched. He had small experience of grandmothers, but he suspected that her ladyship was not of the usual variety. She behaved as though it were an everyday occurrence to invade a man's bedchamber, which for her, perhaps it was. Harry had a notion the lady did as she damned well pleased.

Strolling forward, he drew up a chair opposite her. He had always felt more comfortable with people who behaved in outrageous fashion than those who punctiliously observed all the rigors of a social code.

Lady Dane removed the covers of the silver breakfast service and thrust at Harry a plate laden with muffins, dry toast, eggs, crispy bits of bacon, and deviled kidneys.

"Won't you be joining me?" he asked.

"I breakfasted *hours* ago," she told him loftily.

Harry grinned, but bent over his plate with assumed meekness. As he ate, he was aware of her ladyship studying him over the rim of her coffee cup.

"You have a look of your mother about you," she pronounced. "She came out the same year as my eldest daughter. I knew her ladyship quite well."

"I fear I didn't," Harry said. His mother had died before his third birthday. It saddened him to think he bore not even the most vague memory of her.

"More's the pity," Lady Dane said, some of her sternness melting. "Nan Thorpe was a magnificent girl. The best horsewoman I ever knew. She could manage her men with the same skill as she did her horses. You and your father would have been the better for it if she had lived."

"I am sure we would have." He set his plate aside and waited for her ladyship to come to the point of her visit. She did so with an alarming bluntness.

"Do you love my granddaughter, sir?"

"Yes," Harry replied, equally forthright.

"You still wish to marry her?"

"Very much so."

"Then you have an odd way of going about it. I suppose you thought to pique her interest by pretending to be dead?"

"That was not of my devising." Harry frowned. Yesterday afternoon, he had finally managed to uncover an explanation for his "demise." His death had been reported on the basis of a saber found engraved with his name near a body blackened beyond recognition, the same saber he had tossed to a friend before making that final, fatal charge. Charles had become unarmed, and Harry had still had his pistol.

Leaning back in his chair, Harry briefly closed his eyes, his heart heavy with the memory of that grim moment. He had heard much talk of the glories of battle, but all he recollected was choking on gunsmoke, the terrifying sense of confusion, the thunderous explosions, the screams of the wounded, the searing pain in his shoulder, his horse going down beneath him.

"It must have been Charlie they found with my sword," Harry said wearily, opening his eyes. "When I came to, I had been taken to a convent where some nuns looked after me. I didn't make much effort to communicate to anyone that I was safe, but I never deliberately set out to deceive anyone either." He paused, glancing toward Lady Dane. "Do you think Kate will ever believe me?"

Her ladyship's features had remained noncommittal during his account. She said slowly, "Kate is not an unreasonable girl, but I am not sure it will make much difference whether she believes you or not."

"But she loves me. She could not hide that from me yesterday." Unable to ever keep still for long, Harry rose and leaned upon the back of his chair. "She fainted in my arms, kissed me, gave me a clout upon the ears that was like to take my head off."

"That sounds like a young woman in love," Lady Dane said dryly. "But that doesn't alter the fact that you and my granddaughter are a strangely mismatched pair. I should have never thought to put the two of you in harness together."

A brief laugh escaped Harry. "I wouldn't have either. I must have passed Kate at least a dozen times upon the streets of Chillingsworth and never particularly noticed her. And then one winter evening . . ." Harry sighed. He stalked restlessly toward the chamber's tall windows and stared out at the sunwashed morning. Over the tops of the trees in his park, one could just make out the distant spire of St. Benedict's. But the greenery of summer blurred before Harry's eyes, and he was once more seeing a world blanketed in white, Kate settled before the fire, her dark curls spilling about her face as she bent over his garrick, her eyes shining with a soft light as though all the serenity of the world was to be found centered there.

He had felt like a weary traveler, descending from the wind-blasted heights of some mountain peak and coming across a quiet vale whose stillness had touched his heart.

"As I sat watching her," Harry murmured, "it slowly came to me that . . . that she was beautiful. I think it must have been at that precise moment that I fell in love with her, that I knew my life was never going to mean anything without her."

Harry did not realize he voiced his thoughts aloud until Lady Dane asked, "And so, sir. Did you ever explain all this to her?"

He flushed, forced a smile, and shrugged. "Not in so many words."

Her ladyship nodded with understanding. "Aye, I know. My husband was never a one for making pretty speeches either. But women, foolish creatures that we are, occasionally like to hear them."

"Do you think that pretty speeches would win me Kate?"

"Frankly, no. Is that how you are planning to go about it?"

Harry didn't answer. His chief plan of campaign was to gather up Kate in his arms, capture her lips ruthlessly until she responded in kind, melting against him, but he could scarce confess that to her grandmother.

He didn't have to. The old lady was too shrewd by half.

"That won't answer either, attempting to make love to her all day long," she said, raking him with her keen gaze. "Though I imagine you could make quite a satisfactory job of it. But it will always come down to this. Kate possesses a rock-hard bottom of sobriety. She gets it from her father, though where he came by it, the Lord only knows."

Harry heaved a frustrated sigh. "Then what do you suggest I do? I don't intend to let her slip away from me this time."

"Your only hope, young man, is to acquire an image of respectability. That absurd memorial out there can be put to some use. Let it commemorate the demise of Hellfire Harry."

"Hellfire Harry has been dead for some time," he said bitterly. "Do you think I would have ever presumed to ask Kate to marry me if I had not meant to put my wild days behind me?"

"Apparently you failed to convince her of that." Leaning on her cane, her ladyship rose majestically to her feet. "You may begin this morning by making your appearance in St. Benedict's."

"St. Benedict's!"

"It is a church, my lord, not a debtor's prison."

"I know but—but to try to make Kate believe I have turned into some sort of psalm singer! It seems the worst sort of hypocrisy."

"Not a psalm singer, but a man who understands his duty to God and sets a good example for his people. You cannot expect a bishop's daughter to marry an irreligious dog."

"I would do anything for Kate," Harry said, "slay any dragon but—"

"She doesn't need any dragons slain. She will be more impressed by the sight of you cracking open a prayer book."

Harry opened his mouth to voice another protest, but he felt caught on the crest of a wave, propelling him irresistibly forward. Before he knew where he was at, her ladyship had pulled the bell and summoned his valet to help him dress.

"You have not much time. Services begin in twenty minutes," Lady Dane said, gliding toward the door.

Harry made one last effort to save himself from what he anticipated was going to be an embarrassing and likely futile ordeal. He called after Lady Dane, "You know there is a belief in the village that if Hellfire Harry sets foot inside St. Benedict's, the roof will come tumbling down."

"I am prepared to take the risk," said Lady Dane, calmly closing the door behind her.

The bell in St. Benedict's tower had long since rung its final warning knell as Harry sprinted up the steps. He paused beneath the eight-column portico to catch his breath, leaning one gloved hand up against the church's mottled stonework.

"Hang it all," Harry muttered. Nothing had ever looked more forbidding than the set of massive wooden doors closed in his face. He whipped off his high-crowned beaver hat and brushed back the dark strands of hair from his brow in frustration.

Now what the deuce was he supposed to do? His father had opened many doors to him in his life, the exclusive gaming club at White's, Gentleman Jackson's prize fighting salon, the discreet chambers of many lovely opera dancers. But the governor had never seen fit to initiate Harry as to the doings behind St. Benedict's mysterious portals.

He guessed that those inside must already be deep into the service. Harry grimaced. He would cause enough of a stir simply by entering St. Benedict's without creeping in late as well. Despite what his cousin Julia might think, Harry did not enjoy setting the world by the ears.

He was tempted to turn and slip quietly away again, only held back by a single thought . . . Kate. She was behind that barrier, her face likely stilled into solemn lines as she prayed. For him? Harry doubted it, remembering how they had parted yesterday, the cruel trick she believed he had played. Lady Dane was right. Kisses alone would not be enough to erase such bad impressions.

Harry sighed and took one last self-conscious inventory of his appearance. He was immaculately (and to him, most uncomfortably) attired in bisquit-colored breeches that clung to the outline of his muscular thighs, the forest green coat straining across his shoulders, unbuttoned to reveal the shirt frills peeking beneath a striped waistcoat. The starched cravat with all its intricate folds felt like it was choking him.

Drawing in a deep breath, Harry eased one of the

church doors open a crack, enough to peer inside, his eyes adjusting to the dark stone of the interior. The lancet windows let in not so much as a whisper of breeze on this hot, summer morning. The scent of the flowers adorning the altar hung in the breathless air like a heavy perfume, the rise and fall of the vicar's voice as sonorous as the drone of bees outside the window.

The benches and pews, scarred and venerable with age, held most of the citizens of Lytton's Dene, some of Harry's servants from the hall, and the gentry from the surrounding countryside, like Squire Gresham's boisterous family.

Adolphus made an impressive sight in his vestments, mounted high above the congregation upon the elaborately carved pulpit Harry had heard acclaimed as the pride of St. Benedict's. Harry craned his neck, scanning the pews, but he could not see Kate.

Easing the door open further to slip inside, Harry winced. The ancient hinges groaned so loudly that all the coffins in the graveyard might well have been creaking open to offer up their dead.

No matter how careful Harry tried to be, the door banged closed beneath him with a loud thud. Those on the rear benches were already shifting to see what sinner dared to sneak in after the service had begun. The inevitable astonished whispers followed, and Harry could see some of the good folk actually casting anxious glances toward the roof.

At any other time he might have been amused, but his sense of humor seemed to fail him. Giving a nervous tug to his cravat, he started forward, but no matter how quietly he attempted to walk, his Hessians clattered on the stone floor. Those in the front were now also turning to stare, including his cousin Julia, who cast him a look of blistering reproach.

Harry was beginning to feel like the devil invading the sanctuary of some holy shrine when he spied Kate. She sat three rows from the front, near the aisle, by her mother and Lady Dane. Kate alone appeared unaware of any disturbance, although by this time the astounded Adolphus had floundered, losing his place in the text.

Serenely bent over her prayer book, Kate was wearing one of those old-fashioned gowns that became her so well, a white muslin embroidered with dainty flowers. A cluster of ebony curls peeked from beneath a bonnet trimmed with pink rosettes and a satin ribbon was tied in a demure bow beneath the delicate curve of her chin. Never, Harry thought wistfully, had she looked more like an angel.

She did not glance up until his shadow fell across the pages of her book. Kate emitted a tiny gasp, the volume tumbling from her grasp to land at his feet. Harry bent to retrieve it, handing it back to her with a rueful smile. Two bright spots of color appeared in her cheeks as Harry edged himself beside her on the pew.

"You are in the wrong seat, my lord," she whispered, staring rigidly toward the altar.

Harry spared a glance toward the pew at the very front reserved for the Arundel family, the coat of arms carved on the end. It was unoccupied this morning, for as usual his stepmother had one of her megrims.

"It looks too lonely over there," Harry murmured.

Kate said nothing more, diving behind the protection of her prayer book. Much to Harry's relief, the commotion he had caused died away, all eyes turned back to the front as Adolphus coughed, then shuffled the pages, resuming his place in the service.

But Harry continued to be aware of the stiffness in Kate's frame, noticing how she shrank from brushing up against him. Lady Dane had been wrong, Harry thought, suppressing a sigh. His coming here today had only caused Kate unhappiness and embarrassment.

For her part, Kate could concentrate neither on the pages of her book nor upon what Reverend Thorpe was saying. St. Benedict's was the one place she felt safe from Harry's pursuit. Whatever was he doing here? She knew she had threatened not to be at home when he would call, but surely not even he would seek to foist his attention upon her in church.

She risked one indignant glance at him and was startled to note he appeared as ill at ease as she. Perhaps more so. She tried to remember she had resolved to harden her heart against this man, keep him at a distance. But it touched something deep inside her to see Harry, so strong, so self-assured, looking humbled like an outcast in the very church his ancestors had built.

She nudged his arm. With a mute gesture, she offered to share her prayer book. He flashed a grateful smile that tugged at her heart, although she blushed more deeply when he removed the book from her grasp and gently returned it to her, right side up.

With Harry's sun-bronzed features bent so close to her own, it made an end to any prospect of her deriving benefit from the vicar's sermon. She caught but one word in ten, her gaze straying to the way Harry's dark lashes shadowed his eyes, the sweet, sensitive curve of his mouth, the square, wholly masculine line of his jaw. She felt her pulse quicken. Would she ever be able to study Harry's face again without being drawn to his lips, the memory of his kiss . . . ?

Kate flushed with shame, scandalized by the direction she had allowed her thoughts to take—and in church of all places! When the last amen sounded, she echoed it with relief, feeling the need to put some distance between herself and Harry.

Harry stepped back to allow her to pass by him into the aisle. She was aware of his low-murmured greeting to her mother and grandmother, but Kate kept walking, following the other parishioners crowding toward the door.

Only when she had stepped out into the sunlight of the churchyard did she pause to take a steadying breath. She knew Harry would be hard on her heels, and she turned over in her mind the speeches she had lain awake half the night rehearsing.

My lord, I must insist that we be no more than mere acquaintances. It will be the better for both of us.

Kate nodded. That had a noble ring to it, kind but firm. *My lord* . . . she repeated to herself again, certain that Harry would be joining her at any moment.

But as she glanced back to the church doors, she saw that Harry had been cut off from her by a sea of people. The squire was clapping him on the back and roaring out that St. Benedict's had not known such excitement since the invasion of the Roundhead army. Others . . . mostly ladies, Kate noted with a frown, were wringing Harry's hand and exclaiming over him.

Of course Kate had always been aware how attractive Harry was to the ladies, so handsome in the raffish way most women adored, his smile so winning. But not until that moment did she realize that ever since the night he had crashed into her garden, she was accustomed to his attention being fixed solely upon her.

Not that she was in the least jealous. No, how absurd, she thought, nearly ruining the toe of her sandal by digging it into the dirt. She didn't even have the right to be jealous, having so thoroughly thrust Harry out of her life. And in fact—she crushed several blades of grass beneath her foot—she was relieved Harry was too preoccupied to rush to her side.

Turning her back upon him, she stalked up the steps of the church portico to where Reverend Thorpe lingered. The poor man looked a little forlorn, being accustomed after the service to have most of his flock gathered about him.

"Today's sermon was most . . . most enlightening," Kate said, wincing a little at this polite lie, unable to recall one word of the discourse.

"Thank you," the vicar said, "You are most kind, Miss Towers—"

He was interrupted by Julia bustling up to join them, in time to hear these last remarks. "The sermon would have gone much better without the disturbance," she said, her lovely face marred by a peevish expression. "Whatever possessed Lytton to come here this morning?"

As Julia asked the question, her eyes seemed to bore into Kate. Kate felt her color heighten.

"He likely came to pray," Kate said, struggling to keep the acid tones out of her own voice. "Surely there is nothing so remarkable in that."

"For Lytton, it would be," Julia said flatly.

Reverend Thorpe hastened to interpose. "I was most gratified that Lord Harry came. It seems our cousin has taken heed of my admonishments at last."

Julia shot her brother such a look, Kate half feared she meant to call the vicar a fool. But she merely grated, "You are much too good, Adolphus."

Kate had always thought so herself, that the vicar was virtuous to the point of being a little priggish. But she had been much ashamed of herself for harboring such an unbecoming opinion. As a bishop's daughter, she should have taken more pleasure in the worthy Mr. Thorpe's company. Yet she felt nothing but dismay when Julia extended an invitation for her to dine at the parsonage.

"We could spend a nice quiet afternoon together, just you, I, and Adolphus—"

"Oh, thank you," Kate said, but made haste to stammer out her excuses. She had so many pressing duties, with her grandmama arrived but yesterday. Her mother would be wanting her. Indeed she should have not kept Mama standing about in the heat even this long. Murmuring her farewells, Kate bolted back down the steps. She all but blundered into the squire's hoydenish daughter, Becky.

"Isn't it grand, Miss Towers, having Lord Harry back?" the girl cried happily. "He's such a great gun."

Kate resisted the impulse to glance to where Harry was surrounded by an admiring throng. "It is most pleasant," she agreed with Becky. "But I doubt your mama would care to hear you use such unlady-like expressions."

Becky ignored the reproof. The lively redhead had a knack for hearing only what she wished. She chattered on, "Lord Harry looks ever so smart today. In prime twig. I am glad for he appeared terribly blue-deviled yesterday when he realized his friend must be dead."

"I-I beg your pardon?" Kate asked.

"His friend, Charles Masters. You know, the one his lordship lent his sword to during the battle. That's why everyone thought Lord Harry had been killed, and here the poor fellow himself knew nothing about it."

"What—" Kate began hoarsely. She forced Becky to go through the entire story over again, not an easy task for the girl expected herself to be immediately understood even though she never related any tale in logical sequence.

By the time Becky sauntered off to greet another acquaintance, Kate had pieced enough of the facts together to feel herself go pale. So Harry had not been responsible for the rumor of his own death. He had been as much a victim of the grievous error as anyone else.

And to think how horridly she had treated him . . . Kate pressed one hand to her cheek. But why hadn't Harry told her the truth at once, she wailed inwardly. *He tried to. You wouldn't listen*, her merciless conscience replied.

Kate hung her head. She should go to Harry, apologize to him at once. But if Kate had one failing, her Papa had often admonished her, it was her pride. The bishop had always been so understanding because he bore the same sin himself. It was most difficult to admit when one had been wrong.

She stole a glance toward Harry. He had managed to escape the flock of females but had fallen into the squire's clutches. Gresham was obviously badgering his lordship about selling those hunters. Harry was laughing but firmly shaking his head.

Kate flushed with shame. Overcome with remorse, she felt she could not face Harry at that moment. Quickening her steps, she hastened to where her mother already waited by the gig drawn up in the lane by their sole male servant, John.

To her dismay, Kate discovered that a problem had arisen regarding their transportation. Her grandmother, who had come to church on her own after some mysterious errand, had imperiously dismissed her coach back to the stables.

Lady Dane raised strenuous objections to riding crushed between Kate and her mother in the gig. "Far too crowded for three on a hot day," her ladyship declared.

Kate sighed but offered to walk. She truly did not mind, it being her favorite form of exercise, but Lady Dane also objected to that.

"Nonsense. Your mother would never want you walking in this heat. Would you, Maisie?"

"Well, I—" Mrs. Towers began.

"That settles it." To Kate's horror, Lady Dane turned about and snapped, "Lytton!"

79

"Oh, no, Grandmama, pray don't," Kate faltered, guessing Lady Dane's intent. She hoped Harry might not have heard. But she did not know how it was—Lady Dane never actually raised her voice, yet it had such carrying power.

Across the churchyard, Harry's head snapped up eagerly. Bowing, he managed to escape Gresham, even the squire forced to give way before a summons from Lady Dane.

In several quick strides, Harry crossed over to the gig. Kate averted her face, scarcely knowing where to look. Although Harry addressed her grandmother, Kate sensed his eyes were upon herself.

"My lady?"

"I cannot abide being crowded upon such a hot day. Perhaps you would be so obliging as to fetch Kate home, my lord."

"With pleasure."

"No, I-I must not impose," Kate said. "That is I must call upon . . . upon Mrs. Hudderston. I promised to bring her a recipe for our housekeeper's honey syrup. Little Tom has developed the most distressing cough."

"Then Lytton may take you there as well," Lady Dane said, disposing of his lordship as though he operated a hackney cab. Kate half turned to her mother for support, but she knew it would not be the least use expecting the gentle Mrs. Towers to resist Lady Dane's ruthless maneuvers.

In her flustered state, Kate was never quite certain how she got there, but she found herself being handed up into Lord Harry's curricle. At least, she noted with some relief, he was not driving the high-perch phaeton that Harry knew made her nervous.

It was not until Harry leaped up beside her to take the reins that Kate realized his lordship had somehow dispensed with his groom. If she had not known better, it would almost seem as though Lady

Dane and his lordship were linked in a conspiracy to get her alone with Lord Harry. Kate dismissed the notion at once as being foolish, born out of the butterflies that seemed to have taken up residence inside her.

Harry whipped up his team, setting the chestnuts with their flowing manes into motion. The reins looped about his gloved hands with an easy grace, Harry expertly maneuvered his vehicle past the press of other carriages and wagons exiting from the churchyard.

A silence that seemed more heavy than the still summer air settled over them, until Harry sent the team into a smart trot down the dusty lane. Harry cleared his throat.

"Er—cracking good sermon we had this morning."

"Yes," Kate said faintly. She removed her fan from her reticule, applying it with more vigor than was necessary.

"I always did like that tale about the prodigal son returning. How everyone forgave him no matter how wicked he had been. . . ." Harry's voice trailed off suggestively.

Kate knew this was a perfect opening for her to beg his pardon. She glanced down at her clenched hands, her throat tightening.

Harry startled her by suddenly drawing rein, bringing the horses to a dead halt. A large oak spread its shade over the road, protecting them somewhat from the scorching sun. A mournful-looking cow peered at them over a fence.

"Kate." Harry turned to her. She could not bring herself to look at him. "I am sorry . . . about this morning, I mean."

He was apologizing to her? Kate's remorse deepened until she felt ready to sink.

"I never intended to interrupt the service."

"You don't have to beg pardon for coming to

church, my lord," Kate said. "I thought it was wonderful—"

"No, it wasn't," Harry replied glumly. He started to reach for her hand, barely checking the movement. "I can't deceive you about motives. I only came because of you, because of wanting to see you, hoping you might think better of me. Perhaps you might even like to have me there beside you."

The constriction in Kate's throat tightened so she could scarce breathe. It occurred to her that she had indeed liked having Harry there, too much. As the bishop's daughter, she knew she ought to tell him the only reason for attending church should be his own soul, but she found herself too deeply touched to think that he had altered the pattern of a lifetime simply for her sake.

Swallowing her pride at last, she said in a low voice, " 'Tis I who should apologize to you, my lord. I heard how the report of your death came about, that it was none of your doing."

"Well! That's a great relief." Harry heaved a cheerful sigh. "Though there's nothing for you to be sorry about."

"All those terrible names I called you!"

"Oh, I am sure I deserved them for something or other." Harry peered down at her, hating the distress he saw gathering in her eyes. Plague take it, he would rather he had done what she had wrongly accused him of, than see Kate looking so wretched with guilt.

"But—but you were wounded," she faltered.

"Only a trifle."

"And I hit you. So hard."

"True. You have a most impressive bunch of fives. But I really need to teach you not to lead with your right."

Kate's conscience appeared too stern to allow even one smile to escape her.

"If you are feeling that guilty," Harry said, leaning his face closer, "You may kiss me and make it feel better. Then I shall be only too happy to turn the other cheek."

Kate shrank back. She wasn't feeling that stricken with remorse. "It was partly your fault, my lord," she said, biting down upon her lip. "Why did you never write to tell anyone what had become of you?"

Harry raised his shoulders in a shrug that was perhaps a shade too nonchalant. "I didn't suppose anyone would much care."

"There are a great many people who do." She swallowed. "I-I am quite fond of you, my lord."

"Kate!"

"And I trust we shall always be friends," she added primly.

Harry moved closer, stealing his arm about her waist. "I hope so, too. I know I am considered hopelessly unfashionable, but I think it much better when married people can remain friends."

He saw the flash of alarm in her eyes and knew he was rushing his fences. Though it took a great effort of will on his part, he withdrew his arm. "No need to look so panicked," he said. "That wasn't the beginning of another proposal. I never ask girls to marry me on Sunday."

When she cast him a doubtful glance, he drew himself up with feigned sternness. "It's supposed to be a day of rest, Miss Towers. As a bishop's daughter, you should know that."

An indignant gasp escaped her that turned into a most unwilling gurgle of laughter. "Oh, Harry, you really are abominable."

"That's better," he approved, turning his attention back to his restive horses, giving them the office to start up again. "I thought you were going to 'my lord' me to death."

The team set off down the road, a jauntiness in their step that was reflected in the lifting of Harry's own spirits. True, Kate's response had not been all that he had hoped. She was not ready to cast herself into his arms, but at least he had got her to smile. And Harry had learned to be ... oh, just a trifle more patient than he had been two years ago.

Kate struggled to school her face into a more prim expression, but it was a losing battle. Harry had ever been able to make her laugh when she tried too hard to be serious. He grinned at her and tossed the reins in her lap. Kate caught them in a gesture that was almost reflexive.

"Do you still remember?" he asked.

"Of course I do," Kate said, taking up the challenge, gathering up the leather in a firm, but graceful grip. It was Harry himself who had taught her to handle a team. He watched her critically for a moment, then relaxed back against the seat appearing satisfied with her performance.

It was not an accomplishment of which her Papa would ever have approved, but Kate could not help a glow of pride creeping into her cheeks. Harry did not permit just *anyone* to drive his chestnuts.

As the team followed the winding lane, sweeping past the hedgerows and fields, Kate sensed another distance being closed as well—the span of two years. The constraint she had expected to feel with Harry simply did not exist. It was as though all those lonely, empty days, weeks, months had never been.

She sensed that Harry felt it, too. He loosened his cravat, heaving a contented sigh.

"Lord, it's good to be home. I had nigh forgotten how green it all is here. . . . Nothing has changed," he added softly, looking toward her. She knew from the warmth in his eyes he was speaking of more than his lands.

Her heart gave an answering flutter and she half

started to agree with him. But memory intruded. Something indeed had changed since that spring. There was a freshly laid stone among all other aged memorials in the vast cold halls of Chillingsworth Cathedral.

Kate's shoulders sagged beneath a mixed weight of sorrow and guilt. Harry read the change in her expression all too well.

"I was sorry to hear about your father," he said.

He spoke with a quiet simplicity, and Kate knew that, despite the differences that had existed between himself and the late bishop, Harry meant it.

"Thank you," she murmured. Although Harry had been away in London at the time of her father's death, a spray of flowers had found its way to her door. The enclosed card had borne but one word, *Harry*. Yet somehow that had brought her more consolation than all the scriptural outpourings of her father's ecclesiastical friends.

It had not been long after that she had received the tidings that Harry had bought his commission. Kate had been deeply troubled by this rash action, and she ventured to mention it to him.

"I was worried about you when I heard you joined the army. I was afraid that perhaps it was all my doing—that I was to blame."

"Because I was nursing a broken heart? Nonsense, Kate. You know I have a tougher hide than that. No, it was simply that London was becoming a dead bore and, in any event, it's family tradition. All the Lytton men at sometime or other seem to have gotten a mad hankering to run off to be a soldier." After a pause, Harry said reflectively, "Though I don't know why. Rum business soldiering."

Despite the offhand nature of the comment, something in Harry's tone caused Kate to glance at him. His features had stilled into somber lines, a darkness gathered in the wells of his eyes that Kate had never seen there before. In that instant Kate realized Harry had sustained more wounds at Waterloo than just his arm. So full of life himself, he was not the sort of man to take pleasure in death, not even of his enemies.

She longed to reach out to him, comfort him, but as ever Harry was quick to toss off his own somber mood with a jest. He proceeded to assure her with mock solemnity, "You see me returned home, my Kate, content to live the rest of my life as a sober country gentleman. I intended to become so stuffed with respectability, my tailor shall have to let out my waistcoats."

Kate could not quite prevent her brow from quirking in dubious fashion. Harry began to make all sort of outrageous promises that ranged from attending church every Sunday to never engaging in any sport more dangerous than whist for a penny a point.

Although he had her laughing as they drew near the turning to Hudderston farm, Kate could not forebear remarking, "I hope all this newfound respectability includes showing a greater interest in your estates."

"Oh, indubitably," Harry said, taking the reins from her, guiding the curricle past the stile.

The Hudderstons were some of Harry's best tenants. The wide welcoming barnyard was as well noted for its flock of speckled hens as for its brood of lively, sandy-haired children. The only thing that marred the appearance of the snug, solidly built stone farmhouse was that one end of the thatched roof had through time and neglect begun to sag.

"Lord!" Harry exclaimed in shock as he reined in his team.

Kate half turned to him, not wishing Harry to be too distraught with remorse. After all, he had been away so long, but any reassurance she had been about to give was cut off when Harry emitted a low whistle.

"Damme! But those children have grown several hands since I saw them last. Even little Jack."

So saying, Harry was quick to alight. He handed down Kate and was soon swallowed in a sea of freckled faces. Despite the passage of time, he was somehow still able to identify all the little Hudderstons by name.

Kate could only gape at him as she realized that Harry didn't seem to notice the roof was about to cave in on their heads. She could have shaken him, but it would have taken a far more hard-hearted female not to melt at the sight of Harry tossing a small girl up onto his shoulders, her braids flying amid squeals of delight.

"Oh, Harry." Kate sighed, shaking her head ruefully.

So charming . . . but so irresponsible, just as the bishop had always said.

And even though Kate could not help smiling as she followed Harry toward the house, a string of little ones hanging on to his coattails, she could feel the shadow of her father once more passing between them.

Chapter 6

Dawn broke over Mapleshade, a fine mist shrouding the distant majesty of the towering trees, golden light spilling across the dewy green lawn until it resembled some lush carpet scattered with pearls. Harry peered out the study window, rubbing eyes gritty from lack of sleep.

It was not the first time he had watched the sun come up over his parklands. He had often witnessed this magnificent spectacle after one of those grueling all-night card sessions with his father, or riding home in the wee hours, his head splitting from carousing at one of the inns in Chillingsworth.

This time, however, it was a far different reason that found him out of his bed at daybreak. Wearily, Harry's gaze tracked to the oak desk littered with sheets of rumpled parchment, the candle that was no more than a charred wick protruding from a lump of dried wax. The scene bore mute testimony to his nightlong labors, going over the condition of his estate—a most dismaying and unrewarding task.

Massaging some of the stiffness from his neck, Harry turned back to the far more agreeable prospect that lay just outside his window. He had never been given much to flights of fancy, but his lands, beneath the sun's first rays, bore an aura of enchantment, the mists and soft light conjuring up images of days gone by.

Harry could well imagine the first earl, that dashing cavalier, charging across the lawn toward the Hill, the plumes of his hat waving, his sword drawn in defiance against Cromwell's soldiers, his bold deeds winning for him the heart of his lady fair.

Aye, Harry envied that ancient lord. How easy he had had things. Merely rattle his saber, hold Mapleshade against a score or so of Roundheads, mayhap endure a wound or two, and the woman of his dreamings had melted into his embrace.

"But I'll wager the woman in question was not a bishop's daughter," Harry murmured with a wry smile. Quite the reverse. He had not seen Kate since he had driven her home from church five days ago, and their parting had been far from warm.

He had sensed the change in her immediately after, what had been for him, a most delightful visit to Hudderston's farm. But as he had handed Kate back into the curricle, she had been distant, taking refuge behind the prim demeanor he knew far too well.

When he had set her down at her own gate, she had attempted to fob him off with a stiff handshake. But he had held her fast, summoning up his most engaging grin.

"*Now* what have I done wrong, Kate?"

She refused to answer him, merely looking flustered. Finally he did manage to goad her into saying, "It is not so much what you have done, my lord, as *what you have not.*"

As Harry tried to figure out what the devil that meant, Kate disengaged her hand, blushing deeply. "Forgive me, my lord. I should not— It is not my place to say— Good afternoon and thank you so much for bringing me home."

She had given him a look, at once so sad and somehow filled with disappointment, before fleeing into the sanctuary of her cottage, leaving Harry standing at the gate, feeling more confused than ever.

It was then that he had discovered the advantage of having an ally within Kate's stronghold. Kate might continue to try to avoid him, but not so her grandmama. When he had asked Lady Dane if she knew what had gone awry, that formidable dame did not mince words.

"It's the state of your tenants' farms, you young cawker. Kate feels you haven't been doing your duty by 'em and the heavens forfend! If there was one word that girl *was* taught the meaning of before she could even say 'mama,' it was duty."

At first, Harry had waxed indignant against the charge. He might not be the best of landlords, but as for neglect! He frequently passed by his tenants farms on horseback, enjoyed tousling the curls of the babes, jesting with the men, playfully flirting with their good wives, listening to the grandfathers spin tales of their youth.

But he took enough heed of what Lady Dane had told him to ride back to the Hudderston place and study it through more critical eyes. What he saw caused his face to burn with shame. The plaguey roof was all but coming down upon their heads.

As in turn he examined his other properties, he made discoveries equally as mortifying. To think that Kate must also have noticed all this. No wonder she thought him such a frippery fellow.

Hence his midnight session, trying to sort out the problems of the estate, poring over accounts until his head ached, wondering what was to be done, not quite knowing where to begin. As he had paced before the study window, watching the sun rise, he had at last in desperation sent for his steward.

A soft knock at the door alerted him of Warburton's approach. Harry hastened to settle himself behind the desk, attempting to arrange the papers into a more tidy heap.

"Come in," he called.

The steward crept into the room. Warburton was a thin man, as dry as the parchment sheets of ancient ledgers, his eyes the color of faded ink.

"You sent for me, my lord?" he asked in a hesitant tone.

"Yes, I did."

Warburton looked utterly confounded. Harry supposed he could understand why. In truth, he had scarce ever paid more heed to Warburton than to one of the books in the library, devoting his interest to the advice of his head groom or his gameskeeper.

"Come and sit down," Harry said.

Warburton did so, but he perched on the very edge of his seat as though yet expecting to find that the request for his presence had all been a mistake. His dull eyes drooped from the weight of skin bagging beneath them. Harry experienced a twinge of guilt as it occurred to him that he had dragged the old man from his bed at a most unreasonable hour.

But when Harry apologized, the steward protested, "Nay, my lord, I was awake. It has been a lifelong habit of mine to be up at first light of day."

"Mine as well." Harry grimaced, then moved on to the purpose of the interview. "I have been making a tour of the estate."

Warburton's eyes rounded with even greater astonishment.

Harry tapped a piece of parchment laid before him. "I have compiled a rather long list of matters that need attention."

Warburton stiffened. "I have done my best, my lord, as I have always done—"

"I am not blaming you," Harry interrupted soothingly. "Even a good servant cannot make up for a bad master. I know that in the past I have given you short shrift when you attempted to discuss estate business. The truth is . . ."

Harry trailed off. The truth was that although his father had taught him many things, to ride like the devil, to drive to an inch, to fire a pistol with creditable accuracy, the governor had never done much by way of teaching Harry how to look after the estate. Although he now regretted that circumstance, Harry was far too honest to lay all the blame at the old earl's door.

"I have been an idle and ignorant fellow," Harry concluded instead. "But now I want to take more of a hand with Mapleshade, but I must rely on you for instruction, Warburton. Do you think you could contrive to teach a dull dog like me?"

Mr. Warburton gaped at him for a moment, then said, looking both flattered and disconcerted, "C-certainly, my lord. That is not that I think you are a dull dog, but that if you really mean it, I would be most happy to assist you."

Harry bit back a smile at this flustered speech and assured Warburton he would be most grateful. But in the next few minutes, Harry was not quite so sure. Never would he have guess the dour Warburton could be so voluble.

With an eagerness that bordered on pathos, the steward proceeded to barrage Harry with a stream of facts about land taxes, farm leases, and crop rotation until Harry was laughingly obliged to fling up one hand.

"My dear fellow, I don't think I can quite master the whole of it in one morning. Perhaps we could deal with the most immediate problem. I am concerned about the state of some of my tenants' farm buildings."

Warburton's face fell. As Harry proceeded to outline his plan for repairs to the Hudderston roof, the steward looked downright uncomfortable.

"That would be wonderful, my lord, and I should have seen it to myself long ago." Warburton paused and coughed delicately against his hand. "But for one small problem—the funds."

Harry felt his face wash a dull red. He did not require any further explanation from the steward. His estates had been encumbered with debt when he had inherited them, due mostly to his father's penchant for gaming. Harry had never acquired the governor's taste for the dice and cards, but with a stab of conscience, he realized he had never been good at practicing economies himself, his own particular vices being his horses and an openhanded policy about lending money to friends.

He sighed. "Surely there must be at least enough income to thatch the Hudderston roof."

Warburton said nothing, merely reached for the quill pen and sketched out some estimated figures for Harry.

"That much for a wretched pile of straw?"

"The war caused a shortage, my lord. Perhaps if this year's crops do well and none of the money is drained out of the estate, by next spring—"

"By next spring, the Hudderstons will be using their roof for rushes. There must be some quicker way."

"I suppose you could sell off some of the timber."

Harry thought of the ancient fell of trees that was the crowning glory of his lands. No, he would not figure in the history of Mapleshade as the earl who had cut the timber. Neither did he find Warburton's next suggestion any more palatable.

"Raise the farm rents? That would be worse than a window tax, and a little like asking the Hudderstons to pay for the privilege of having a hole in their roof."

Warburton spread his hands in a helpless gesture. "Then I don't know what other remedy remains, my lord."

Unfortunately, Harry did. The thought came to him with the swiftness of a sword thrust and just as piercing. He tried to resist the notion, but he feared the longer he dwelled on the prospect, the less likely he would be able to act upon it.

"I know of another way to obtain the necessary money," he said quietly. He offered Warburton no explanation, but reached for the quill with grim purpose. He scrawled out a note which he sanded, folded, sealed and handed to Warburton.

"See that this is delivered to Squire Gresham."

"Oh, my lord. Not your hunters!"

Harry attempted a careless shrug, but could not quite manage it. "No sense having a pack of horses eating me out of house and stable. I daresay I shan't have much time for hunting in any case."

Warburton accepted the note, but he regarded Harry with a new light of respect in his eyes and a sympathy that made Harry uncomfortable. Harry turned away, adding gruffly, "I suppose if one means to do a thing, there is no sense of going at it by halves. The chestnuts may go as well. I am meeting my old friend, Sam Ffolliot in the village this afternoon. I am sure he would offer a fair price."

"Mr. Ffolliot!" Warburton choked in dismay.

When Harry regarded the steward from beneath upraised brows, Warburton flushed.

"That is, I have heard tell the Honorable Mr. Ffolliot is a most amiable gentleman. . . ."

Harry grinned. "Folly is a complete ass, but he takes good care of his horses."

Within days of his return, Harry had been besieged by an invitation from the honorable Samuel.

Folly meant to race his footman against Lord Erwin's, laying a monkey on the outcome. Even if Harry did not wish to place a wager, he might just want to come along and crack a bottle or two with the fellows.

But such pleasures had long ago begun to pall for Harry. All too frequently he had found himself yawning behind his hand and checking his watch. Somehow he seemed to have outgrown his former companions. Perhaps falling in love with Kate had done that. His stint as a soldier had surely finished it.

Yet he could not bring himself to completely snub his old friend. Of a certainty, Folly had far more hair than wit and Harry had hauled the man out of more than one scrape. But there was no real harm in him, no trace of that streak of meanness that characterized Harry's other erstwhile companion, Lord Erwin. Thus Harry had agreed to pass at least the afternoon with Folly at the Arundel Arms in the village. The meeting would serve a double purpose if he could persuade Folly to buy the chestnuts.

Having reached his decision, Harry refused to dwell on the sale of his horses any further, wanting neither pity nor praise. Instead he engaged Warburton in a discussion of how the money thus raised could best be spent, a talk that moved on to some schemes the steward had been perishing to set into motion for many a day that would improve the future income of the estate.

Harry could not say that the morning sped by. When he arose from the desk, he felt curiously more drained than after a hard day on the hunting field. But he carried away with him a satisfied feeling of having accomplished something.

It did not surprise him when he received a reply from Squire Gresham as early as that same afternoon. In his eagerness to close the deal, the squire had sent along not only the necessary bank notes, but a groom to fetch away the horses.

Harry had reconciled himself to the loss of the hunters, but he did not feel particularly enthusiastic about watching them being led away. Directing the squire's man toward the stables, Harry betook himself to another part of the house to change into his riding clothes for the meeting with Folly.

Before he departed, he thought he might as well see to another grim duty and be done with it—that of his daily inquiry after the state of his stepmother's health. Ever since his return, Sybil had kept to her rooms. Their initial reunion had proved disastrous, Harry's continued refusal to receive Lucillus Crosbie causing Sybil to collapse in tears. Although he remained adamant, Harry did his best to make it up to her in other ways.

As he passed through the long gallery that contained the portraits of his ancestors, he half fancied that from within their gilt frames, those raffish gentlemen regarded him with amused sympathy, from the first bold cavalier to that bewigged rogue who had been Harry's grandfather.

The line of portraits stretched unending until recent times, where naught but a bare panel remained. The spot where the last earl should have been was empty. It filled Harry with regret that his father had ever been too restless even to sit for his own painting, leaving Harry with nothing more to remember him by than recollections of some rollicking good times.

And Sybil.

Harry drew up outside the door to his stepmother's sitting room. Squaring his shoulders, he knocked, but not too loudly, lest Sybil accuse him of giving her a headache before he even set foot in the room.

He waited for the familiar quavery response, but nothing but a heavy silence greeted him from the opposite side of the portal. After a moment, he thought he detected a hushed whispering and then a scuffling sound.

Harry knocked again. "My lady?"

More scuffling and then renewed silence.

Harry frowned. Headaches be dammed. He knocked louder this time. "My lady, is anything—"

"Ohhh." He was cut off by a low groan. A weak voice bade him enter, an unnecessary command for Harry was already pushing the door open.

He paused on the threshold, half fearing he might find Sybil going off into one of her swoons. She was indeed reclining on a gilt Egyptian-style sofa, her usual posture, but not in her usual attire. Even by this time of day it was nothing to find Sybil still in curl papers, her dressing gown draped about her ample form.

But although she lay upon the sofa, one hand flung over her eyes, her brassy curls were arranged neatly beneath a lace cap, and she was attired in a sprigged muslin gown that would have looked quite charming on someone thirty years younger.

"Oh, Harcourt," she said. "What are you doing here? I thought you had gone out riding."

Was it his imagination or did Sybil seem even more dismayed than usual to see him? Harry started to answer her, then recalled Sybil did not like anyone 'shouting' across the room.

Closing the door as softly as he could, he inched forward, taking care to avoid an étagère crammed with bric-a-brac. Ever since he was a lad, his stepmother's sitting room had always made him edgy, every available surface cluttered with fragile china objects. He never failed to break a piece of it, sending Sybil off into paroxsyms of tears, while he slunk guiltily away, the evidence of his crime clutched in his hands.

"I came to see how you are getting on today," he

said, "before I ride into the village. If there is anything that I can do for you—"

"No, nothing. Nothing at all." Sybil stunned him by the brightness of her smile. She fidgeted nervously with the gold filigree bracelet banding one plump wrist. "Do run along, my dear boy. You are looking positively piqued. I am sure you must be wanting some fresh air."

Never could Harry recall being Sybil's "dear boy" or her showing solicitude for the state of his health. Harry eyed her dubiously and wondered what might be in the latest medicine she was quacking herself with. He moved to examine the small table at her elbow, only to be brought up short. The familiar tray with its array of smelling salts, headache powders, and assorted strange bottles was missing.

In its place was a teapot, cups, and saucers—two sets of them to be precise. At that same moment, Harry caught a whiff of a familiar, cloying odor. Lavender water. Sybil had many faults but dousing herself with scents wasn't one of them.

Harry's eyes narrowed dangerously, but he concealed his suspicion and sudden flare of anger behind a tight-lipped smile.

"It is good of you to be so concerned about me," he said, strolling about the room with forced casualness, his gaze darting here and there. Most of the furniture in the room was as dainty as Sybil's china, with elegant scrolled arms and legs. The only area of the parlor that afforded any place of concealment was . . .

Harry glanced toward the open window, the brocade drapery billowing every so slightly with the summer breeze. At the curtain's hemline Harry could just make out the toe of a boot.

"But fresh air does not seem to be my problem," Harry continued. "In fact, I think I am taking a chill. If you don't mind, I'll just close the window."

"No," Sybil shrieked, sitting bolt upright. But Harry was already striding toward the casement. In another second, he had collared the slender young man hiding behind the draperies, dragging Lucillus Crosbie from his place of concealment.

Crosbie was a good-looking youth, his waves of light brown hair flowing past his ridiculously high shirt points. His dreamy eyes, which most of the ladies declared so poetic, now bulged with alarm.

"L-lord Lytton," he gasped, struggling to free himself from Harry's grasp. "Please don't do anything hasty. I can explain—"

"No explanations are necessary. I thought, upon one another occasion, I had made my feelings about your calling upon her ladyship perfectly clear."

"You did, sir, but—" Crosbie paled as Harry tightened his grip. "Oh, pray, not the pond again!"

"Nay, I wouldn't dream of so disturbing the fish."

Before Crosbie could say another word, Harry hefted him off his feet and tossed the fellow out the window. Crosbie's own startled howl was only eclipsed by Sybil's scream.

As Harry slammed the window closed, she flung herself across the room, pressing both her hands and face against the glass.

"Oh, Harcourt. You—you ruffian. You have dropped poor Mr. Crosbie into the rose bushes."

"Blasted careless of me. Roses are so damned hard to grow."

Harry glared out the window himself, watching Crosbie struggle painfully to his feet. Although he risked a longing glance at Lady Lytton, the fellow possessed enough sense to limp away from the house.

Striding into the hall, Harry shouted for one of the footman to make certain Crosbie found his way off the property, also snapping out, "Tell Gravshaw I want a word with him."

His once redoubtable manservant was getting confoundedly careless about whom he let through the front door. It would be much easier to vent his exasperation with Gravshaw than return to deal with Sybil.

Harry did not relish having to preach propriety to anyone. Considering his own past, it made him feel ridiculous. But damn it all, Sybil was his stepmother. No matter how foolish the woman was, he couldn't stand idly by and let a jackanapes like Crosbie make a cake of her.

When he returned to the sitting room, he half feared to find Sybil already sunk into hysterics. Instead she stood silhouetted by the window, drawn up into a dramatic pose that would have done credit to a Sarah Siddons.

"Harcourt! You are entirely too cruel."

"I don't call it cruel to try to protect you from the havey-cavey intentions of Lucillus Crosbie."

"Lucillus is a gentleman. He wants to marry me."

"He's a dashed—"

"Don't shout!" Lady Lytton pressed one hand to her brow. "Your voice goes right through my poor head." She staggered to the sofa and began searching behind the pillow for her smelling salts.

Harry had not realized he was shouting. It was amazing how Sybil always found his voice too loud when he was saying something she did not care to hear. He continued doggedly, "Crosbie is a dashed fortune hunter—"

"He is not! You don't know him. He has the sweetest nature imaginable." Sybil paused long enough to uncork the bottle of sol volatile and take a fortifying sniff. "He is willing to consign my widow's jointure to perdition if that is what it would take to convince you of his good intent."

"Is he indeed? And what the deuce would the pair of you live upon?"

"Lucillus has prospects. He is a brilliant sculptor."

Harry rolled his eyes.

Sybil thumped her plump fist angrily against the sofa. "Even you said the statue for your memorial was well executed."

"Yes," Harry grudgingly conceded, "but in questionable taste."

"That wasn't Lucillus's fault. He was obliged to use a statue of Apollo he had already designed. He merely changed the head and substituted a sword for the lyre. It was remarkably clever of Lucillus and a great savings as well."

"You mean you obtained my memorial secondhand?" Harry asked in a slightly unsteady voice.

Lady Lytton bristled defensively "The tidings of your death came at very short notice, Harcourt. I managed the best I could."

"S-so you did." Harry's lively sense of the ridiculous overcame him. Despite how hard he tried to control it, a bark of laughter escaped him.

Her ladyship eyed him reproachfully. "I never thought even you could be this unfeeling, Harcourt. When you were named as trustee of my jointure, I never said a word, though I did think it most odd, that a child should be given such control over the parent. But I trusted you to behave reasonably. Never did I think . . ." Both of Sybil's chins quivered. "You wish to see me a human sacrifice. Buried alive with your father."

Harry sobered immediately. "No, I don't. Believe me," he added with great feeling. "*No one* wants to see you remarried more than I. But not to a court card like Crosbie. Damn! For you to be setting up a fool like that in my father's place. It's an insult to his memory."

Sybil's face colored, her cheeks turning the same bright red as her rouge. "No one respects your father's memory more than I. I have been a good widow, but I am far too young to go on . . . I hate black and Lucillus is not a fool. ..." Her tangled speech trailed off into incoherency, the inevitable flood of tears commencing.

As she sobbed tragically into her handkerchief, Harry watched her in acute discomfort. He hated making anyone so miserable, and there was nothing more odious than being told that something was being done for one's own good.

But any temptation he might have felt to yield was checked by the memory of those final hours he had spent at the old earl's bedside. His father had known he was dying, but he wanted no clergyman about him, only Harry and his pack of hunting dogs. The governor had no fear of death and no regrets about the way he had lived his life save one.

"I should have never married again," his father had confessed to Harry. "There was only ever one woman for me, my boy and that was your mother. Poor Sybil. I've been the very devil of a husband to her. The foolish creature has not a whit of sense or she never would have had me. It's going to be up to you to look after her when I'm gone, Harry."

Harry's throat tightened at the memory. It was the only thing the old earl had ever asked of him, the only responsibility he had ever laid upon Harry's shoulders. There might be little else in his life he had ever done right. Surely he could manage to fulfill his father's one simple request.

Harry's conscience pricked him just a little, for he knew it was not only the old earl he was thinking of, but Kate. Good lord, what would she think of him if he was so careless of his duty as to permit his stepmother to wed some silly chubb half her age?

Nay, even though he was disturbed by Sybil's gusty weeping, Harry remained resolved. He made one more effort to console his stepmama, patting her awkwardly on her shoulder.

"I tell you what I will do, my lady. At the end of

the summer, I will convey you to Bath. You've always enjoyed taking the waters, and the town would be full of more eligible suitors."

"Old men with the gout!" was Sybil's wailing response to this hopeful suggestion. Recognizing the beginning of some strong hysterics, Harry prudently backed toward the door. He suddenly realized that this was the first time he had entered Sybil's room without breaking any china, but he did not expect his stepmother to take much consolation in that at the moment.

Wearily, Harry turned and let himself out.

Julia Thorpe unfurled her parasol, shortening her longer stride to match Kate's as they strolled through the village of Lytton's Dene. Miss Thorpe, as ever managed to present a crisp, fresh appearance, despite the heat and dust coating the lane.

Kate could not help recalling a laughing remark Harry had once made about his cousin's cool elegance. "Aye, icebergs don't easily melt."

As for herself, Kate could already feel her curls damp with perspiration beneath her bonnet, and her muslin gown clung to her as shockingly as though she had deliberately dampened her petticoats. She wondered what possessed her to be ranging abroad on such a hot afternoon, except that she had decided she had been keeping too close to the house of late. She had been nowhere since last Sunday and was beginning to feel quite out of touch with the world.

"With the world?" a voice insider her jeered. "Or with Harry Arundel?" It was quite true she had neither seen nor heard from Harry since their abrupt parting at her gate. Her manner had not been such as to encourage his lordship to call again. Perhaps she had convinced him at last to abandon his pursuit of her. Perhaps he had simply found something more interesting to occupy his time.

In either event, she told herself, she felt relieved that Harry had ceased to plague her, although her relief had taken on a most strange form, leaving her feeling restless, starting at every knock upon the cottage door, flying to the window to gaze out at every passing rider.

Such nervousness, however, Kate had convinced herself, had nothing to do with Harry's absence. No, more likely it was to be blamed upon the vicar's sister, for although she had seen nothing of his lordship, she had seen far too much of Julia these past days.

Even now as they skirted past Mr. Rising's carpentry shop, the smell of wood shavings and the clang of hammers heavy in the air, Julia seemed all too oppressively close to Kate's side.

"It is far too hot to be out walking," Julia complained. "I declare we both must be quite mad."

Kate forebore to remind Julia that she had not been invited along upon this expedition. It had been Julia who had insisted upon accompanying her.

"If you are feeling unwell," Kate began hopefully, "and wish to return to the vicarage, I would quite understand—"

"Nonsense. My dear Kate, I would not think of abandoning you." Julia gave her one of her arctic smiles, and linked her arm through Kate's in a possessive manner Kate found nigh suffocating. The thought flashed through her mind that now she knew how prisoners in gaol must feel, so closely guarded. She dismissed the notion at once as mere peevishness, borne out of the heat and irritation of nerves.

"So where is it that you wish to go?" Julia asked after the manner of an adult humoring a tiresome child.

"I had thought of calling in at Miss Lethbridge's."

Kate indicated a small pink-and-white brick shop with some bonnets displayed in a bow-front window.

"Why ever would you want to go in there? That wretched woman trades in nothing but gossip."

Kate had to agree, and as a bishop's daughter, of course, she had no use for gossip. All the same she heard herself replying, "Miss Lethbridge has acquired a length of brown merino that I am thinking of purchasing to have done up into a winter cloak."

Julia made no comment, but her opinion was expressed clearly by the supercilious fashion in which she arched her brows. But she followed Kate to the shop across the lane without further demur.

The interior of Miss Lethbridge's shop was small and close, the narrow shelves crammed with an odd assortment of fripperies, laces, ribbons, gloves, bonnets, and stockings that comprised the elderly spinster's stock in trade. The establishment was empty when Kate and Julia entered, Miss Lethbridge folding up the silk fringe she had failed to sell to her last customer.

The diminutive woman summoned up a polite smile for the vicar's sister, but she bustled out from behind the counter to greet Kate with enthusiasm.

"The brown merino, Miss Towers? Bless you, my dear, I shall fetch it in a trice."

Hurrying to one of the lower shelves, Miss Lethbridge dragged out a bolt of cloth that she displayed to Kate upon the counter.

"A good serviceable fabric, my dear," the shopkeeper said.

Kate half-heartedly examined the ugly fabric that was the exact shade of the mud that filled the lane after a hard rain. She was aware of Julia close at her elbow, the lines of her face taut with a kind of bored impatience. It roused a rare streak of perversity in Kate, and she took her time about studying the fabric, although she wondered herself why she persisted in lingering when she had no intention of making a purchase.

As usual, Miss Lethbridge's tongue ran on at such a breathless rate of speed, she was oft unintelligible. Kate listened in desultory fashion, having no interest in the latest prank of the squire's hoydenish daughter or how the butcher's boy had been caught stealing a slab of bacon.

But the shopkeeper's next remark caused her to glance up eagerly in spite of herself. "I beg your pardon, Miss Lethbridge. What did you say about Lord Lytton?"

Miss Lethbridge blinked, her bright inquisitive eyes rounding in surprise. "Why, nothing, my dear. I merely remarked that if you did wish to buy the cloth, I would have it sent to your cottage. On such a hot day, you surely wouldn't be wanting to *carry* it."

"Oh," Kate said faintly, a rush of embarrassment flooding into her cheeks. Beneath Julia's sharp stare and Miss Lethbridge's look of motherly amusement, Kate felt ready to sink beneath the floorboards.

It only made matters worse when Miss Lethbridge patted her arm. "Bless you, child, there's no need for you to color up so. I am sure all the young ladies hereabouts are fair starved for some word of Lord Harry. I have been telling everyone—"

"I assure you," Julia interrupted icily, "neither Miss Towers nor I is prey to any such vulgar curiosity."

Kate knew she should agree with Julia, but she felt more like stuffing a kerchief in Miss Thorpe's mouth. Miss Lethbridge appeared affronted.

"I do not consider it vulgar to show a friendly concern for one's neighbors," she huffed. "But far be it from me to be burdening you with any tales of his lordship. The poor lamb." Miss Lethbridge heaved a deep sigh before briskly setting about to refold the bolt of brown cloth.

It was entirely too much for Kate. Despite Julia's look of disgust, Kate put her hand timidly over Miss Lethbridge's to still the woman's movements.

"Oh, pray, Miss Lethbridge. Whatever did you mean? Why did you call the earl a poor lamb?"

Miss Lethbridge's lips were compressed in a taut line, but when she glanced up at Kate's face, her expression softened.

"Why, only that I think there must be something gravely amiss with his lordship since he's come back. He's done naught but a little gentle riding over his own estates, nothing at all in his usual dashing style. There's some as have been saying that Lord Harry was wounded more badly at Waterloo than any of us know."

"Surely not," Kate faltered.

Miss Lethbridge nodded solemnly. "Why else would the earl sell off all his best hunters? 'Tis obvious the poor gentleman must not be able to ever hunt or jump again."

"Harry sold his hunters?" Kate cried, aghast.

"What utter nonsense," Julia broke in, abandoning her pose of disdainful disinterest. "Lytton prizes his precious beasts above rubies. Never would he part with them."

"That is where you are quite out, Miss Thorpe," Miss Lethbridge said, her thin features flushing with triumph. "For not an hour since, I saw the squire's groom leading those horses through the village. Paid a wicked high price for them, the squire did. I cannot imagine what Mrs. Gresham will say to him." She added slyly, "Though I am surprised that any of this is news to you, Miss Thorpe. You being his lordship's cousin and so thick with him as you are forever telling everyone."

Julia sucked in her breath with a sharp hiss. Turning a cold shoulder upon Miss Lethbridge, she said to Kate, "If you are quite finished here, Kate, I should like to go."

"Yes, I am ready," Kate said, although she wanted nothing more than to remain and ply Miss Lethbridge with a dozen more questions, even with Julia's critical gaze fixed upon her. But it was obvious the shopkeeper had already told her all she knew about Harry.

But why would Harry sell off his most prized possessions? Harry had never given a fig for the consequence of his title, his vast estates, or acquiring great riches. But his horses! Kate had seen him care as tenderly for their well-being as a father would his babes. She could not imagine what dire circumstances would have induced Harry to part with them.

So unsettled was she by these unexpected tidings that Kate ended by purchasing the ugly brown cloth, though she scarce realized what she did. She quit the shop with a worried frown creasing her brow, all but forgetting Julia's presence.

Miss Thorpe was quick to remind her. "That insufferable gossiping creature," Julia said as soon as they had gained the street outside. "But there! She is typical of the incivility and lack of gentility to be found in this wretched village. I am only astonished that you should have encouraged her, Kathryn."

"I only wanted to know—" Ruefully, Kate bit down upon her lip, for once feeling far too disturbed to be guarded in Miss Thorpe's presence. "Julia, why do you think Harry has sold his horses?"

"Heaven only knows. Lytton is forever in some sort of scrape."

Kate found this reply far from reassuring.

"I am far more concerned about you, Kathryn," Julia continued.

"Me? Why?"

"You display a most unseemingly interest in Lytton's doings." Julia regarded her through narrowed eyes. "You have not been so foolish as to fall in love with my cousin, I hope?"

Kate glanced quickly away, willing her color not to rise. "Of course not."

"I am glad to hear it. Lytton is a sad rake, you know."

"He is not!"

Julia's eyebrows rose. With great effort, Kate lowered her voice. "That—that is, I know Lord Harry can be a shocking flirt, but there is such a kindness in him. He would never set out to break any lady's heart."

"He is my cousin, and I believe I know him far better than you," Julia began angrily, then checked herself. She forced a smile to her lips, "But, my dear Kate, let us not fall into a quarrel over him. It is far more attention than Lytton deserves, I promise you. It is only the heat that is making us both so cross and—" Julia broke off with a look of extreme annoyance. "I have left my parasol in that wretched woman's shop. If I do not retrieve it at once, I would not put it beyond her to sell it to her next customer."

Julia clearly expected Kate to return with her, but Kate made no move to do so. After muttering in vexed tones that she would catch up to Kate, Julia strode back toward Miss Lethbridge's. Kate had to suppress a strong urge to bolt along the lane and thus escape Julia's oppressive presence. She was growing weary of Miss Thorpe's sharp tongue, her repeated attacks upon Harry.

It seemed to Kate that she displayed little cousinly regard for his lordship, rather callously dismissing Miss Lethbridge's speculations that something was gravely amiss with Harry. Could the shop-keeper be right in her surmise about the severity of Harry's wound? It would be just like him to conceal such a thing from everyone.

Scarce heeding where she walked, Kate strained to remember every detail of her outing with Harry the previous Sunday, every expression upon his face. Never had he seemed more hale and yet . . . Upon further recollection had his movements seemed not quite so quick as usual? And yes, Kate was certain that she recalled him turning away when he had lifted her down from the curricle. To conceal a grimace of pain perhaps?

With such alarming thoughts chasing through her mind, Kate did not realize she had wandered too far out into the lane until she was alerted by the thunder of hooves, a blast of a horn. Blowing upon his yard of tin, a coachman was urging the afternoon stage toward the inn yard of the Arundel Arms.

The team of four sweating horses was bearing down upon her. Kate froze in momentary panic. Her heart leapt into her throat, but before she could make a move, she felt strong arms dragging her to safety.

Kate spun about colliding with the hard wall of Harry's chest as the stage rattled past. His arms banded about her, crushing her so tightly she could feel his heart thudding as hard as her own. He swore at her.

"Damn it, Kate. What on earth did you think you were doing?"

She shook her head, unable to answer him at first. She had no notion whence Harry had sprung, only feeling grateful that he was there, even if he did huskily call her "a little fool" and hold her far too close.

For a moment all Kate could do was lean weakly against him, soothed by the comforting feel of his arms about her. But as her fright subsided, she became all too conscious of her position, being embraced by Lord Harry for all the village to see.

Drawing in a steadying breath, she pulled away from him, gazing up at his face. All thoughts of her own near calamity fled, her mind returning to the worries that had so troubled her earlier.

She scrutinized his features more earnestly than she had ever done before. He looked haggard, deep lines of exhaustion carved about his eyes, stealing away the smile from his lips. She feared it was owing to far more than his recent concern for her safety.

"Are you all right, my lord?" she asked.

Harry's grim expression vanished. For a second he appeared nonplussed, then his features broke into his familiar irrepressible grin.

"Am I all right?" he laughed. "The woman nearly flings herself beneath a coach and then asks if I am all right?"

"I mean . . . are you quite well?"

"Well enough, although I would be a dashed sight better if you did not choose to wander about in the midst of the road. What the devil possessed you, Kate?"

"I fear I was woolgathering."

Harry arched one brow wickedly. "Daydreaming about me?"

"It so happens that I was. . . ." Kate started to confess, then stopped beginning to feel a little foolish. She was not about to admit to Harry how she had permitted her imagination to run away with her. For it was patently obvious she had done so. Harry might bear an appearance of fatigue, but his swift rescue of her and a quick perusal of his hard muscular frame demonstrated there was naught in the least amiss with his body. Kate wrenched her eyes away, heat stealing into her cheeks. She longed to simply ask Harry about the hunters, but how could she do so without revealing she had been gossiping about him with Miss Lethbridge?

"I was admiring the bonnet," she finished lamely, "in the window across the way and not watching where I was going. I but came into the village to do a little shopping."

"For your bride clothes, I hope." Roguish lights danced to Harry's green eyes as he caught her hand, brushing a playful kiss against her fingertips.

Kate tried to summon a reproving frown, but could not quite manage it. Even that fleeting contact of Harry's lips sent a breathless, tingling kind of rush through her.

"It isn't Sunday anymore," he reminded her. The rogue's light vanished, the warmth in his eyes becoming more intense. "Will you marry me, Kate?"

"N-no. Oh, Harry, please." She made a weak protest as he upturned her hand and placed a not so chaste kiss upon her wrist, the heated contact seeming to sear her flesh.

"M-my lord, you mustn't," Kate cried, attempting to disengage her hand, casting a flustered glance about her. Her distress must have been evident enough for Harry released her at once.

"I am sorry, Kate," he said. "I had no intentions of trying to make love to you in the middle of the road. 'Tis only that you cannot imagine how much I have been missing you these past few days."

So where have you been, she had an urge to demand. But to do so would be to admit, even to herself, how much she had been missing him.

Kate fussed with her bonnet, straightening it, attempting to regain her composure. "And what brings you to the village this afternoon, my lord?"

Harry's lips twitched, and Kate suspected that he regarded her with a kind of tender amusement. But he replied solemnly enough, "Well, besides keeping damsels from straying beneath coach wheels, I have come to meet an old friend, Miss Towers."

Kate saw no sign of a mount or Harry's curricle. Dear heavens! Had he sold all his horses?

"You came on foot?" she asked.

Harry looked rather surprised. "Of course not. I rode Ramses."

Kate sighed with relief, which only caused Harry's expression of puzzlement to deepen.

"I left Ramses at the stable over at the inn where I was to meet Folly," he explained. "But the dratted fellow is never on time."

"Folly?"

"Yes have you never met him? He lives not far from Chillingsworth and I am sure— Ah, well, never mind, I shall introduce you, for here he comes at last."

Turning, Harry raised his arm and proceeded to hail the driver of a gig who was tooling into the village at a spanking pace. He was on the point of sweeping past, but at Harry's call, the gentleman sharply drew rein. Kate stepping back to avoid the spray of dust, waving her hand before her eyes.

"Folly, you idiot," Harry choked.

It took Kate's vision a moment to clear before she could make out the form of Harry's friend. Her first impression was of a dapper young man wearing a curly brimmed beaver, his clothing protected by a riding cloak with a multiplicity of capes. He was, Kate supposed, what she had heard vulgarly referred to as a 'buck of the first stare.'

It was only when Harry began to perform the introductions and the man swept the hat from his glossy waves, that Kate obtained a clear view of an amiable and familiar countenance. She stiffened with the recognition.

"The Honorable Samuel Ffolliot," Harry was saying. "And this is—"

"Mr. Ffolliot and I have met before," Kate said in clipped tones.

"I daresay not," Mr. Ffolliot replied jovially. "Not likely I should forget such a pretty lady."

"It was at the episcopal palace in Chillingsworth. My father was the late bishop of that diocese."

Mr. Ffolliot regarded her with polite bewilderment, his wide innocent eyes appealing to Harry for enlightenment, but Harry was obviously equally at a loss.

A hard knot burned in Kate's throat. To think that this fool did not even remember the incident that had nigh broken her father's heart.

"It was upon the occasion that your pistol shot shattered the stained glass in the Blessed Lady chapel."

"Oh, Lord!" Kate thought she heard Harry mutter under his breath, but she was too caught up in the painful remembrance to take much heed. She could still see her father's shoulders bent with grief as he stood surveying the colorful shards that had once been a magnificent representation of the Madonna and child, one of the few examples of fourteenth century stained glass to have survived both the ravages of Henry the Eighth and later, the Puritan army.

Mr. Ffolliot scratched his head, then a shading of guilt pinkened his cheeks. "Oh, yes, now that you mention it, I do remember something of the sort." He offered Kate a deprecating smile. "But truly, I meant no harm. I suppose I must have been fox— er that is, I was having a little trouble with my vision that day—and it was only a wager."

Kate set her face into grim lines, offering him no hope of pardon, so he appealed to Harry. "I did pay to have the window replaced—with some nice new glass, you know, which I am sure would have been much better than that old stuff that had to have been there for ages."

"Four centuries to be exact," Kate said tersely.

Mr. Ffolliot beamed. "There! That is just what I meant—"

"Oh, do be quiet, Folly." Harry grimaced, casting an uneasy glance at Kate. "What's done is done. There is hardly anything to be gained by raking over old coals."

Her entire frame rigid with reproach, Kate did not agree with him. Such wanton destruction as Mr. Ffolliot had caused could not be so easily forgiven or forgotten. What gave her more pain than anything else was to discover that Harry could be friends with such a man.

An uncomfortable silence settled over the three of them, only to be broken as Julia at last came down the lane seeking Kate. Never had Harry shown such relief to see his cousin.

Vaulting up beside Mr. Ffolliot, he strongly suggested that the ladies be left to pursue their shopping, his haste to get Samuel away quite evident. With a final tip of his hat to Kate and Julia, Mr. Ffolliot started up his mare, heading toward the inn yard.

Kate turned away immediately, ignoring the rather anxious smile that Harry offered her in parting. Julia fell into step beside her.

"I am sorry that I took so long, Kathryn," she said. "But that foolish woman had already put my parasol in a 'safe place' and then the creature could not recollect what she had done with it. But I daresay Lytton and his friend kept you agreeably entertained?"

Kate made no reply to this rather barbed question, quickening her pace. She only wanted to return to the peaceful sanctuary that was her cottage and indeed was wishing she had never left it.

"Lytton seems to have wasted little time in seeking out the old set."

Kate knew she should simply let Julia's remark go unquestioned. If Miss Thorpe had anything to say about Harry, it was generally unkind. But Kate could not seem to help herself.

"Old set?" she asked.

"His old circle of friends, Ffolliot, Lord Erwin, and the others. All of them quite wild and quite foolish. Did you never hear of them?"

"No," Kate said, feeling quite numb with misery.

"I daresay even Lytton would not have brought such disreputable company with him when he visited the bishop's palace." Julia added, on a note of almost malicious amusement. "In any event, now we know why Lytton was obliged to sell of his hunters."

"We do?"

"It is obvious. He had to pay off gaming debts."

"No!"

"My dear Kate, what do you think Lytton and his friends do of nights for entertainment? They scarcely sit about, reading scripture to each other."

"I-I . . ." Kate faltered, feeling herself go pale. But she managed to rally. "I am sure I scarce gave the matter any thought, being no concern of mine. Now let us make haste. It is almost teatime, and I am suddenly feeling most fatigued."

She set off at a brisk pace, but Julia, with her longer legs, had no difficulty in keeping doggedly at her side.

Julia experienced a mild sensation of triumph. Ever since she had seen Lytton drive off with Kate last Sunday, she had been experiencing all manner of alarm, the apprehension that her own scheme for marrying Kate to Adolphus would come to naught. She had attempted to keep as close a watch as she could over Kate these past few days, subtly pointing out his lordship's defects whenever opportunity availed.

But never had she felt that she had delivered a master stroke until now. She pressed home her advantage, now bringing up the subject of her brother, praising all his manifold virtues.

"And he is so shy," she said as she and Kate turned

in at the cottage gate. "I fear he has developed a tendre for you, yet his modesty prevents him from speaking. Of course, you know that nothing would give me greater joy than to have you as my sister."

"Indeed," Kate murmured wearily.

It vexed Julia to realize Kate had likely not heard a word she had been saying. A rebuke sprang to her lips only to be stilled as she studied Kate's face. In her eyes lurked an expression of such deep-set misery that Julia was moved to a rare stirring of pity.

She had become fond of Kate, as much as she was capable of being fond of anyone. She was shrewd enough to guess that Kate was indeed in love with Lord Lytton, and it caused Kate great unhappiness to believe that he could be a hardened gamester.

Guilt niggled at Julia for she was aware that despite all his other inequities, Harry had no taste for gaming.

Yet he could have changed, she argued with herself. Besides he had enough other faults to make him unsuitable as a husband for Kate. And as for love, Julia had never experienced such a tender emotion herself, but with a little fortitude on Kate's part, it could be easily dismissed.

Thus quieting her conscience, Julia followed Kate into tea. Before she had passed into the cottage, she had suppressed the twinge of sympathy and convinced herself that she was acting in the girl's best interests. By the time she had done with Kate, not only would she abandon all tender feelings for Lord Lytton, Kate would quite sensibly learn to despise the man.

Chapter 7

The shadows had lengthened across the parlor by the time Miss Thorpe took her leave of Kate. Mrs. Towers was glad to see the cottage door close behind that icily bred young woman. She did not know what the vicar's sister had been whispering to Kate, only that Kate listened with little pleasure.

In point of fact, Mrs. Towers could scarce recall having seen Kate look more dejected and miserable, not even in those days following the bishop's death. She had appeared serene enough when setting out for her walk earlier. Mrs. Towers strongly suspected that something had gone awry during that little expedition to the village, and that something most likely had to do with Lord Harry.

But when she ventured to ask Kate if anything troubled her, Mrs. Towers received the usual reply.

"You must not worry about me, Mama," Kate was quick to answer, following it up with a brisk hug. The affection was there, Mrs. Towers thought sadly, but so were the protective walls forever closing her out.

Supper proved a dismal affair with Kate saying too little and Lady Dane saying too much. Her ladyship appeared in none the best of humors either, scolding Kate for getting too much sun "traipsing about all afternoon with that Thorpe chit."

By the time the meal had ended, Kate pleaded a headache and tried to escape to her room, but Lady Dane insisted they all retire to the parlor. Mrs. Towers tried to intervene on her daughter's behalf, but as usual her gentle objections were swept aside.

"I have a gift I wish to present to Kate," her ladyship insisted.

Kate had no choice but to precede Lady Dane into the parlor. She sat stiffly upon the settee regarding with lackluster eyes the elegantly trimmed bandbox that her ladyship presented to her.

"I did not have that sent all the way from London merely for you to stare at it," Lady Dane said, nudging the box closer to Kate with the tip of her cane. "Open it."

Sighing, Kate slipped off the ribbon and removed the lid to reveal a ball gown cut on the latest and most fashionable lines. As she shook out the folds of white India gauze shot through with silver and delicate pink silk applique, Mrs. Towers exclaimed with delight, but Kate regarded the gift with no more than dutiful politeness.

"Thank you, Grandmama," she said in wooden accents.

"I ordered that frock for you from my own modiste," Lady Dane said with great satisfaction, seemingly oblivious to Kate's lack of enthusiasm. "I daresay it will require a few alterations, but my maid Hortense can see to that. She is clever with a needle as all these Frenchwomen are. I am sure she can have it finished in time for the assembly tomorrow night."

"I never attend the local assembly, Grandmama." Kate folded the gown carefully and returned it to the box.

"Then 'tis high time that you did."

"My papa would never have approved. He did not

think it seemly for the bishop's daughter to be seen at a public dance."

"But you are no longer the bishop's daughter."

Although Kate flinched at this tart reminder, her lips set into that expression of prim obstinacy that Mrs. Towers knew all too well. She stole a glance at Lady Dane's equally determined features.

"Oh dear," Mrs. Towers thought with a sinking heart. She reached nervously for her embroidery from her needlework basket, making a timid effort to change the subject that was ignored.

"There is no reason why you should not attend the assembly under my chaperonage," Lady Dane continued.

"That is very good of you, Grandmama, but I do not *wish* to go."

"Nonsense. A little dancing would do you good. You should see to it that the girl gets out more, Maisie."

"Why, I - I . . ." Mrs. Towers began, quite disconcerted by this unexpected attack. But she had no need to proceed before Kate leapt to her defense.

"It is not in the least Mama's fault. I have been too busy for such frivolous pursuits as dancing."

"Busy!" Lady Dane was far too elegant to snort, but the sound that she made came perilously close to it. "Busy with what may I ask? Exactly what have you been doing with yourself, child, buried here in this dismal village for the past year?"

"Many things." Kate lifted her chin proudly. "Receiving callers and . . . and visiting the sick of the parish—"

"That task should rather fall to that Thorpe female," Lady Dane said. "She is the vicar's sister, is she not?"

"Julia is not always . . . disposed to such work. As a matter of Christian charity, I felt that I—"

"Charity is all well enough," her ladyship interrupted. "But one bears a duty to one's own family."

"I have always looked after Mama," Kate cried.

"Indeed! Kate is a most attentive daughter." But Mrs. Tower's faint interjection went unheeded.

"You have other duties, my girl," Lady Dane said. "The foremost being not to saddle your mother with the care of you till the end of her days. 'Tis time you thought of marriage."

"Oh, pray, don't," Mrs. Towers protested. Kate looked so stricken by her grandmother's harsh words, that for once Mrs. Towers actually thought of telling Lady Dane to be silent. Instead she said, " 'Tis not as though Kate . . . she is scarcely yet on the shelf."

"She will be if she continues to dillydally," was her ladyship's inexorable reply. "The child is no longer in mourning. It is time Kate met some eligible young men. If there is not any particular one hereabouts she wishes to marry, then I shall insist that she comes to London for the Season."

"That will hardly be necessary, Grandmama." Kate rose from the settee, the color flying in her cheeks, her eyes overbright. "I shall attend the assembly if that is what you wish. I never intend to be a burden to my family. I hope that I will always know my duty."

With that noble speech, Kate gathered up the bandbox with the air of an ancient Christian martyr going to face the lions and fled from the room.

As soon as her daughter had gone, Mrs. Towers shot to her feet, gripping the back of an armchair with trembling hands. Rarely had she ever dared contradict her mother-in-law, but her umbrage at Lady Dane's callous treatment of Kate could not be contained.

"You were far too hard upon her." Mrs. Towers

quivered with indignation. "How could you make her feel as though she were no longer wanted in her own home?"

"Do sit down, Maisie. I have no patience for such sentimental piffle." When Mrs. Towers did not immediately comply, Lady Dane fixed her with her eagle's eye and sharply rapped her cane. "Sit down if you please!"

Mrs. Towers didn't please, but she sank back into the chair, despising herself for a faint heart.

"Some sternness with the girl seems wanted. My other tactics have not worked thus far." Lady Dane scowled. "I shall have to have another word with Lytton. Whatever can the boy be about? He should be more attentive, nosegays and that sort of thing, not leaving Kate alone for days on end."

Mrs. Towers wished Lady Dane would leave both Lord Harry and Kate alone, wished even more for the courage to tell her so. She said, "I still fail to see how being cruel to Kate can remedy the situation."

"It is not cruel to appeal to the only thing the child comprehends, her sense of duty. You know she loves the boy. We simply have to find the way to overcome her ridiculous scruples."

Mrs. Towers did not find bullying Kate a proper method, but Lady Dane talked heedlessly on, weaving her own plans. "I shall make sure Lytton attends that assembly as well." Her ladyship chuckled. "A little waltzing in the arms of that handsome young man and, you mark my words, Kate will leap forward most eagerly to embrace her 'duty.' "

"Kate doesn't waltz."

"Then I shall find her a dancing master."

Mrs. Towers stifled a groan, sagging back against her chair.

Lady Dane unbent enough to offer a consoling nod. "You must not fret so, my dear Maisie. I have raised four daughters, all of them as muddleheaded as your

Kate, and I guided every last one of them into successful marriages. Depend upon it, I'll wager Kate is even now coming to her senses and deciding that she will have Lord Harry."

Long after the rest of the household had lapsed into the peaceful stillness of night, Kate tossed and turned upon her feather tick pillows. Sleep was impossible with the events of the day crowding forward into her mind—that disastrous encounter with Harry in the village, Julia's acid whisperings about him, but most especially the disturbing conversation she had had with her grandmother.

You are no longer the bishop's daughter . . . what have you been doing with yourself . . . your duty to marry.

Kate rolled over, stuffing her head beneath the pillow, but she could not seem to shut out that insistent voice. At last, despairing of finding any repose, Kate rose from her bed and slipped on her wrapper. Lighting a candle, she left her bedchamber and made her way through the silent house.

Kate scarce knew what drew her toward the tiny front parlor. Perhaps because it was the one room in the cottage that retained an aura of her father's presence. Sadly, she trailed her fingers over his marble busts, the bookcase that housed all the bishop's ponderous texts.

Never had she missed her father so keenly as she did tonight; never did she feel in such want of his wisdom. Setting her candle upon the mantle, she gazed upward, trying to draw some consolation from the portrait of the serene and saintly looking man mounted so far above her, but disturbingly, the bishop seemed to stare back at her with Lady Dane's eyes, full of stern reproach.

What have you been doing with yourself this past year?

Kate averted her head, as though to avoid that too piercing gaze. Aye, she had been quick to justify herself to her grandmother earlier, but standing before her own merciless conscience, Kate could find no satisfactory answer. The months all seemed to have evaporated like the mists of a dream. She vaguely recalled those numb, empty days after her father had died, packing away their belongings in the palace, moving to the cottage at Lytton's Dene.

And after that, her hours had fallen into a routine of of . . . Kate winced, seeing clearly now all the little tasks she had manufactured, tasks to give herself some sense of importance, something to do while she waited. . . . She sagged down upon the settee, her struggles against the realization no longer of any avail.

She had spent the last year of her life waiting for Harry to come home.

"No! No, I didn't," Kate said, but the whisper sounded feeble in the room's unrelenting silence. She hugged one of the settee cushions to her breasts as though that soft silk could somehow shield her from the truth.

Aye, she had flattered herself that she had been so sensible, sending Harry away, avowing that she could never be his bride. Yet had her foolish heart not always kept on hoping that someday, somehow she would be able to give Harry a different answer?

What had she expected? Kate wondered bitterly. Some sort of a miracle? Harry's return from the dead had indeed seemed like one, but the fates conspired again most cruelly to show her that the bishop's daughter and Hellfire Harry were worlds apart. The neglect of his lands, seeing him in the company of that dreadful Ffolliot man, hearing the tale of how he had gamed his horses away—all of that should have been more than enough to convince Kate that her Papa's warnings against Harry had been justified.

And *still* she did not want to believe anything bad of Harry. Still she feared that if he gave her that smile that seemed to draw her straight to his heart, if he asked her again to wed him, she would want to fling herself into his arms with a resounding yes.

"What am I going to do, Papa?" Kate murmured. How could she end this torment? Even if she went away from Lytton's Dene, Harry could always follow her. How could she put herself forever beyond temptation?

The answer came to her unbidden with the memory of Lady Dane's harsh words, *'Tis your duty to marry.*

If she were betrothed to another man, Harry could no longer continue to tease her. He could not keep proposing to a woman who was pledged to another.

The thought seemed to settle in her stomach like a lump of cold lead, but Kate had never been shy about embracing her duty, no matter how painful the prospect.

However Lady Dane's suggestion of repairing to London for the Season would not do at all. No, Papa would never have approved of that. He had always said that the city was filled with naught but rackety young men like Har—

Kate was quick to suppress the unhappy thought, concentrating on the sort of man the bishop would have wished her to wed. A scholar, a man of sound moral principle, sober, steady, a man very like . . .

Adolphus Thorpe.

The mere notion of the solemn vicar made Kate quail and long to dive back to her bedchamber, pull the covers up over head. She promptly felt ashamed of herself for this reaction.

Why not Mr. Thorpe? she adjured herself. Had not Julia strongly hinted that the vicar harbored an affection for Kate? Kate had never glimpsed any sign of such emotion upon Mr. Thorpe's impassive face, but Julia likely knew her own brother's heart far better than Kate.

Adolphus was so handsome, so virtuous, so . . . so *worthy*. As the vicar's wife, her life would be filled with peace and respectability, fraught with useful purpose.

But no love, no laughter, no breathless expectation of something delightful waiting just—

Kate pressed a hand to her brow as though to quell this dampening reflection. She must put all such nonsense out of her head. Her consolation must be that she was at last acting with wisdom.

She knew that Julia and her brother would attend the assembly tomorrow night. Kate would also go, just as she had promised her grandmother. If she discerned any evidence of partiality in Adolphus Thorpe, Kate meant to offer the bashful clergyman every encouragement to ask for her hand.

The resolution brought her little comfort, but at least she now felt exhausted enough to return to her bed. Back within the confines of her room, she snuffed out the candle and burrowed wearily beneath the coverlet.

Yet no sooner had she closed her eyes than Harry's face appeared to her with haunting clarity. He seemed to stare at her, but with no reproach, his laughing green eyes merely sad.

"I have made the wisest decision for both of us. Indeed I have," Kate nearly cried aloud. She rolled over and managed to dispel Harry's image from her mind. But it took her much longer to banish the feeling that her 'wisdom' was somehow betraying them both.

Chapter 8

The night seemed spun from black velvet, the moon a silver disk suspended in the sky. The heady scent of the last of the summer roses drifted through the open windows of the assembly rooms that adjoined the Arundel Arms.

Scarcely large enough to afford space for more than a dozen couples to stand up in comfort, the hall was thronged with its subscribers, mostly the gentry of the surrounding countryside.

The candlelit scene bore none of the dazzling grandeur of a London ballroom, the gowns worn more often of muslin than silk, wreaths of flowers taking the place of flashing gemstones. Yet what was lacking in grandeur was made up for in enthusiasm as the orchestra began to tune their instruments.

Only Kate was able to keep her toes from tapping at the first scrape of the violins. Never had she felt less like dancing, her dainty kid slippers seeming weighted with lead.

"Smile, child," Lady Dane chided her. "You've come here to enjoy yourself, not pay a visit to the tooth drawer."

Kate made an effort to appear more light of heart, all the while wishing herself at home snug in her bed. It had been one thing to form her noble resolve regarding Adolphus Thorpe in the security of her own parlor, quite another to actually prepare to act upon it.

She felt shamefully relieved to note that the vicar and his sister were not yet present. Kate's gaze constantly strayed toward the arched doorway, her pulses fluttering with trepidation. But it was not the Thorpe's arrival that comprised her chief dread, but the possibility of a certain other gentleman's appearance. She had no reason to suppose Harry ever frequented the assembly, but he had a penchant for doing the unexpected, scattering her best-formed intentions like a hurtling ball toppling ninepins. One smile, one laugh, one touch of his hand and all her wisdom had a way of flying out the window.

But not tonight, Kate promised herself. Even if Harry did come, she would greet him with the distance and decorum Papa would have expected of his daughter. Unconsciously she stiffened her shoulders. As she did so, she caught a glimpse of her reflection in the window's night-darkened panes.

Who was that strange young woman that hovered like some unhappy phantom behind the glass? Kate scarce knew herself. Her grandmother's French maid had fussed and primped, decking Kate out in the new gown with its high waistline emphasizing the soft curve of her breasts. Instead of the simple flowers Kate was accustomed to wear for adornment, Lady Dane's diamond necklet glittered about her throat. Hortense had caught up Kate's hair from its loose flowing style and arranged it in a mass of curls pinned up to form a chignon, a gold diadem banding her forehead after the Greek fashion.

Never had she looked so elegant, so stylish. Never had she felt so miserably self-conscious. But she did her best to smile at the young gentlemen who flocked to her side, begging to lead her into the dance.

Other young ladies might have preened themselves at being so sought after, but Kate accepted the situation with gravity. She was not unused to such attention. She had never wanted for a partner at any of the sedate parties she had attended. But she had oft suspected that all those eager young clergyman had stood up with her out of duty or ambition to please her father. Now she supposed it was her fashionable new gown that attracted the gentlemen.

Only Harry had ever sought her out for herself alone. To him she had not been the bishop's daughter, but simply Kate. And when he had danced with her, the world had seemed to fall by the wayside. Caught up by the night and music—

Kate's fingers tightened about the fan, nearly crushing the delicate silk as she fought off the poignant memory. She needed no such recollections to haunt her for she would not, *must not* dance with Harry tonight. As though he had indeed risen up before her, reaching for her with that too beguiling smile, Kate began to promise her dances with a recklessness that bordered on panic, even engaging to waltz with Lieutenant Porter, a newly commissioned naval officer she scarcely knew. Should Harry arrive, he would find Kate with every dance already pledged.

Feeling as though she had erected somewhat of a defense, Kate breathed out a deep sigh. She had actually begun to relax when the vicar and his sister arrived. Kate recalled her purpose in coming to the assembly, and her tensions coiled anew.

The Thorpes edged forward into the hall, Julia and Adolphus resembling nothing so much as a magnificent pair of Dresden china figurines with their matching fair hair and celestial blue eyes. While Mr. Thorpe paused to greet the squire and several of the important landowners of the district, Julia's gaze swept the crowded room with icy disdain. When she caught sight of Kate, she bore purposefully down upon her.

"Kathryn Towers! Such an agreeable surprise." Julia extended both her hands, catching up Kate's by way of greeting. Miss Thorpe's skin was as cool and smooth as silk, leaving little warmth in her grasp. "You did not tell me you were coming here this evening."

Julia's statement hinted of accusation as though Kate had a duty to keep Miss Thorpe informed of all her movements.

"I did not realize that I would be here myself until the last," Kate said. Carefully she disengaged her hands from Miss Thorpe's possessive grip. Julia's eyes skimmed critically over Kate's attire. For once she nodded with approval.

"You look quite *à la mode*. Such a pleasant change."

Kate thanked her for the rather dubious compliment. She supposed she should respond in kind, but she doubted Julia needed to be told how lovely she looked. She was easily the most beautiful woman present, attired in a gown of mauve and white silk, with a long train that proclaimed she had no intentions of dancing.

"There is nothing more tedious than having one's toes trampled by a parcel of provincial clods," Julia said. "I only attend these dreary assemblies because they seem to amuse Adolphus. I do hope you have saved a dance for him?"

Mindful of her own plans regarding Mr. Thorpe, Kate had done just that, but she felt strangely reluctant to tell Julia so. Yet Julia did not wait for her reply. Miss Thorpe turned and beckoned imperiously to where her brother had lingered by the punch bowl to exchange a few words with the squire. "Adolphus, do come here and tell Kate how well she looks."

Kate thought the vicar appeared a trifle vexed by

Julia's summons, but if so, he concealed his annoyance behind a polite smile.

As Mr. Thorpe approached, Kate unfurled her fan. She plied it nervously, wishing it were large enough to hide behind. She had never felt flustered in the vicar's presence before, but neither had she ever considered him as a prospective suitor.

"Good evening, Miss Towers," he said.

"Good evening," Kate murmured, at last daring to look up at him. Her pulses immediately stilled. There was nothing in Mr. Thorpe's mild blue eyes to make even the most giddy maiden feel all of a flutter. If the vicar adored her as Julia claimed, Kate thought dubiously, he certainly did not wear his heart on his sleeve.

"Do say something about Kate's gown," Julia prompted her brother. "Does she not look lovely?"

Mr. Thorpe said all that was required of him and Kate thanked him, her somber manner matching his own. The conversation threatened to lag until Julia said, "Adolphus, you must claim Kate's hand for the next dance before all her other admirers descend upon her."

"Well, I—" Mr. Thorpe began.

"And dearest Kate, you must accept him."

"Well, I—" Kate began.

"How charming. Then that is all settled."

And so it seemed to be, although Kate's mind whirled, scarce sure who actually had made the invitation or who had accepted it. She felt a real sense of relief when Julia moved off to speak to another acquaintance, a relief Kate was astonished to catch reflected in the vicar's own eyes.

They exchanged a half-guilty, half-embarrassed smile that vanished as quickly as the fleeting feeling of kinship. He offered her his arm to lead her to the head of the set that was forming.

The vicar was such a stiff young man, Kate rather expected his movements to be as wooden as a marionette's. To her surprise, he proved quite a graceful dancer, although he was inclined to apologize for his skill.

"I daresay you are thinking the worst of me," he said as they circled each other, "for taking such pleasure in so worldly an activity."

"Not at all," Kate assured him. "Even my father was fond of an occasional quadrille."

Heartened by receiving the late bishop's approval, Mr. Thorpe abandoned some of his formality. Away from Julia, he appeared to have no difficulty in carrying on a conversation. His manners were unaffected and gentlemanlike, his discourse as serious as Kate could require. Kate tried to listen earnestly, but her thoughts kept straying.

She studied the vicar's face and caught herself looking for some resemblance to Harry. But the cousins could not have been more unlike. Kate supposed Adolphus would be judged the more handsome, his skin smooth and unblemished, yet Kate could not help thinking his face might be much improved by some of those fine lines that laughter had carved about Harry's eyes.

Kate quickly dismissed such thoughts as frivolous. As she and Mr. Thorpe came together in the movement of the dance, she realized with dismay he must have asked her a question and patiently awaited her reply.

"I beg your pardon," she said blushing, "but I fear I did not quite hear you."

"It does not matter." Mr. Thorpe heaved a melancholy sigh. "Julia says that I have a habit of forever prosing on."

"Then Miss Thorpe is quite unkind," Kate retorted without thinking. In a flash of insight, it occurred to her that outside of the pulpit Mr. Thorpe was likely not given much encouragement to speak his views by his clever and sharp-tongued sister. Knowing how discomfitted Julia frequently made her feel, Kate experienced a rush of sympathy for the vicar.

"Pray do continue," she urged him. "I am most interested in what you have to say." Quite forgetting the notions of marriage that made her so awkward in his presence, Kate resolved that at least she would accord the poor man some attention. She gazed up at Mr. Thorpe, her smile inspired only by kindness.

But the gentle expression did not escape Julia Thorpe's notice from her vantage point near the doorway. Having snubbed Lieutenant Porter's impertinent offer to dance with her, Julia had stationed herself where she could keep her brother and Kate under constant observation.

Noting the way Kate hung upon Adolphus's every word, Julia's mouth thinned into a smile of triumph. Praise the Lord! Her brother was doing something right at last. She had been admonishing him forever to make an effort to charm Kate, nigh despairing that he would heed her advice.

At this distance, she could not tell what utterances fell from Adolphus's lips, but Kate was clearly captivated. Hereinafter, Julia supposed she must accord her brother a new respect. She had been quite right to believe that the sensible Kathryn needed only a little encouragement to forget her foolish infatuation with Lytton. Although Julia was not given to let her imagination run riot, she could not help calculating how long it might take before the banns of her brother's marriage to the bishop's daughter would be cried. A year perhaps for the wedding to take place, for Kate's powerful relatives to secure Adolphus a better position, for all three of them to be gone from this dreary little village.

These agreeable reflections were disrupted as she

was jostled by a latecomer arriving in the assembly hall. Julia turned to haughtily rebuke the oaf who was even now removing his high crowned beaver hat, revealing familiar waves of glossy coal dark hair. He flashed one of those lightning quick smiles that could send the most surly of lackeys scurrying to do his bidding.

"Lytton!" Julia exclaimed in the same accents of dismay and bitter loathing she would have said 'Lucifer.'

Her cousin tossed off his cloak to the porter tending the door before turning back to Julia with his customary infuriating good humor.

"Julia, you must not act so overjoyed to see me. You know how people love to gossip."

"What are you doing here?" she said, her face flushing with disappointment and rage.

"You are forever asking me that," Harry complained. "I begin to think you are surprised to see me anywhere outside the regions of hell."

" 'Tis where you belong—" Julia choked off the retort, groping for the remnants of her frigid dignity.

Harry chucked her lightly under the chin. "Don't put yourself into a taking, my dear coz. I have not come here tonight to dance with *you*."

He smiled at Julia's gasp of outrage and moved on his way, fully aware of her looking such daggers at him, he fancied he could almost feel the sharp points pricking his back. He supposed he ought to be ashamed of himself for ruffling Julia's feathers, but he was surely entitled to a little amusement.

It had been a most unamusing day. More dreary accounts to be gone over with Warburton, more hysterics from Sybil over that Crosbie fellow, and once again no opportunity to see Kate. The only thing that had sustained him had been the missive he received from Lady Dane, commanding him to attend the assembly. Kate would be present, her ladyship assured him, and possibly in "a more receptive mind regarding the subject of marriage." Harry had his doubts on that score. Kate had looked far from receptive at their last parting when he had dragged Folly away before the blasted idiot could say anything more to affront her. Still Harry held enough confidence in Lady Dane that he conjured up an agreeable image of Kate awaiting him, seated demurely at her grandmother's side, refusing all invitations to dance until Harry should arrive. Her hair would be tumbled about her shoulders in those long silky ringlets, her dress one of those sweet flowing frocks that made her look as though she had stepped from a portrait by Gainsborough.

Harry's spirits raised a trifle at these delightful imaginings, and he edged his way through the crowded assembly with impatient step. Taking no heed of the dancers or other acquaintances who greeted him, Harry sought out Lady Dane.

Her ladyship was not difficult to find. Ensconced in one corner like a queen holding court, she kept the local ladies at an awed distance. When she espied Harry, she frowned and summoned him, her gesture rife with a most royal displeasure.

Harry inched his way toward her and made his leg, but before he could speak, Lady Dane hissed at him, "Impudent rascal. Where have you been?"

"I had some difficulty with my horse," Harry began. The old cobbie he had been obliged to employ now that his chestnuts were gone had raised great objection to being hitched to the curricle. As Harry had helped the groom to quiet the vile-tempered beast, the nag had given Harry's arm a savage nip that left him with quite a swelling bruise.

"I am not talking about tonight," Lady Dane said

with a rap of the ever-present cane. "I mean all this past week, sirrah!"

"I have been buried up to my eyebrows, trying to set my properties to rights. You did bid me become more respectable."

"I said respectable, not dull!"

Harry felt his good humor slip a notch. It seemed unjust for her ladyship to rake him over the coals when he had simply been doing his best to follow her advice. He decided it might be better to let the subject drop.

"Where is Kate?" he asked instead. "You told me she would be here."

"No," her ladyship said in a voice of withering scorn. "I summoned you here to dance with me. Of course, Kate is here, you young cawker. And you'd best look sharp before she is snatched from under your nose."

Her ladyship's acid remark made little sense to Harry, but when she prodded him with her cane and gestured toward the dancers, Harry turned obediently. He eyed the couples promenading in the center of the room, his gaze flitting from one pretty face to another without interest. He vaguely recognized most of the chits present except for the elegant dasher with the Grecian headdress.

Harry took a closer look, then sucked in his breath like a bunch of fives had delivered a punishing blow to the stomach. Kate! It could not be—but it was, her dark hair done up in that style that was all the rage, the white silk gown clinging revealingly to her sylphlike frame. As lovely as the ensemble was, it robbed Kate of that piquant charm that was all her own, making her look like any of half a dozen other society misses rigged out by the dressmaker's art.

"What have you done to her?" Harry groused at Lady Dane in bitter disappointment.

"What have I done with her?" her ladyship asked

in ominous accents. "You might better worry what that yellow-haired dolt dancing with her is now doing."

Harry angled another glance at the dance floor. Amid the swirling dancers, it took him a moment to ascertain which was Kate's partner. When he did, he shrugged.

"Why, 'tis only my cousin, Adolphus."

"The *Reverend* Mr. Thorpe," Lady Dane corrected him. "A perfect match for a bishop's daughter or so I have had to listen to all these old tabbies about me atwittering. If Kate has come to think so, too, it will be all your own fault."

"My fault?" Harry choked.

"For dillydallying. I did my best for you, giving the child a good lecture, telling her it was her duty to marry."

"Saving your ladyship's pardon, but that was a perfectly buffleheaded thing to do," Harry said indignantly. "I don't want Kate casting herself at me out of duty."

"Then you need not worry, because she does not appear to be flinging toward you at all."

Harry thought Lady Dane was raising a dust over nothing, but her remarks were beginning to make him a little uneasy. He made his way closer to the lines of dancers, studying Kate and Adolphus through narrowed eyes.

As the pair met, circled, and parted again, a heavy scowl settled upon Harry's brow. If Kate had been fluttering her fan, outright flirting with his cousin, he could have borne it. But, nay, her eyes raised to the vicar's held no trace of the coquette, only such a gentle expression, her smile so sweet, Harry felt a red-hot brand twist inside of him, searing him with a jealousy such as he had never experienced before.

It was not fair. He could have easily dispatched any other sort of rival. He could outride, outshoot, outfight anyone within the country for Kate. But she did not judge men by such criteria. When it came to the matter of dreary respectability, Harry was painfully aware that, next to Adolphus, he was a lightweight. The vicar would have met the late bishop's approval with a vengeance, and Kate had to be realizing that. Harry's wretched cousin was not exactly hard for a woman to look upon either.

"I should have offered the living at St. Benedict's to that other fellow," Harry muttered beneath his breath. "The one with the wart on his nose."

Damme! It was intolerable. The last of Harry's patience snapped. He had attended church; he had worked on a set of musty books when he would have far rather been kissing Kate; he had given up his most prized horses and then been bitten by a vile-tempered knacker's ware into the bargain. After all that, he'd be damned if he was going to lose Kate to some . . . some *vicar*.

Harry had a strong urge to stride forward and drag her away from Adolphus, but he checked his temper enough to keep from causing an uproar. He waited for the set to finish, grinding his teeth until they ached, his arms locked over his chest.

As the strains of the dance faded to silence, Harry watched his cousin lead Kate from the floor. Was it his imagination or was there already something proprietary in the way Adolphus linked his arm through Kate's?

Pressing his way past the other couples retreating from the floor, Harry followed after Kate. Adolphus was on the point of surrendering her to her next partner, a cheerful young lieutenant whom Harry recognized as Frank Porter.

The vicar was the first to notice Harry's approach. The fellow, damn his eyes, actually had the impudence to hold out his hand and look rather pleased to see Harry.

"Why, Cousin Harry—"

"Lord Lytton to you," Harry grated.

Adolphus's smile faded to one of consternation and bewilderment. "Er - certainly, my lord. This is a most unlooked-for pleasure to see you here this evening."

"Evidently." After delivering this unmistakable snub, Harry rounded on Kate. "Good evening, Miss Towers."

Kate started at the sound of Harry's voice, so deep, so close to her ear, the voice she had been half dreading, half hoping to hear all evening. Her heart skipped a beat. She felt grateful that she had a moment to school her features before she turned to face him.

She managed a rather unsteady, "Good evening, my lord." Risking a glance at him, she stood frozen. She thought herself familiar with every expression of Harry's, from his devil's grin to that warm steady gaze that was always her undoing.

But never before had she seen this unsmiling look that rendered his swarthy features so harsh, the deep furrows by his mouth for once not stemming from laughter.

His voice had a most unsettling edge as he said, "I have come to claim my dance."

"Alas, I—I fear you come too late, my lord. My dances are all bespoken."

"The next dance is mine." Harry reached for her hand, a dangerous glint in his eyes.

A sensation of inexplicable alarm spread through Kate. "Why, Harry, I—I, no, indeed, my lord. You are quite mistaken. I—"

Harry's hand locked about her wrist, tugging her toward the dance floor.

"I say, Lytton, this is is the most barefaced piracy I have ever witnessed." But Lieutenant Porter's good-natured protest was lost as Harry pulled Kate out to the center of the floor.

So much for Kate's plan of defense. She might have known Harry would do something this outrageous. The thought of resisting entered her mind, only to be dismissed. People were already turning to stare.

Yet Harry's action bore none of the mark of his usual teasing mischief. She sensed a suppressed anger about him. Although she could not begin to guess its cause, his dark mood frightened her a little.

"You are being most uncivil, my lord," she said in the sternest voice she could muster.

"I have never been noted for my social graces, Miss Towers."

As the strains of a waltz sounded, he yanked her hard into his arms. Kate let out a gasp that was part outrage, part alarm. But she had no choice but to set her feet into motion, following where Harry led.

As he whirled her in a circle, he continued in that sneering tone that was not Harry's and that Kate felt she could rapidly learn to hate. "You seemed less than delighted to see me, my dear."

"You—you took me by surprise. I did not notice you arrive."

"Very likely because you were too busy making calf's eyes at my cousin."

Kate flinched as though he had struck her. Never had she known Harry to say anything so deliberately cruel. Yet it gave her a startling clue to his anger. Was it possible Harry could be jealous? It seemed the most likely answer. Her plan to marry the vicar and put an end to Harry's pursuit had appeared so simple a solution. What a witling she had been to think that Harry would stand idly by while it happened.

She longed to return a sharp answer to Harry's caustic remark, but much to her annoyance, a flood tide of guilty color rushed into her cheeks.

Harry's mouth thinned to a taut, white line. "Ah, so I see there *is* another reason for your continued refusals of my offer of marriage. Do you expect me to wish you joy, Kate? I will see Adolphus planted in his own churchyard first."

"You are being ridiculous, my lord. If you wish me to continue this dance, pray speak of something else."

As though he sensed her urge to break away, Harry tightened his grip upon her hand. She could feel the heat of his other palm against the small of her back, seeming to sear her through the filmy gown. Kate stumbled slightly. She had but learned to waltz only that morning, and dancing with Harry was nothing like her practice with the dancing master her grandmama had produced. The willowy Mr. James had not been so rock hard, nor had he looked ready to eat her alive. Harry's gaze dipped down the front of her gown, and his scowl assumed an even blacker hue.

"Where the devil did you get that frock?"

"Grandmama gave it to me," Kate said, raising her chin with more defiance than she felt.

"I detest it," he growled.

"I did not wear it with any thought of pleasing you, my lord." Kate felt her own temper stir. "I expected you to be seeking some less mild diversion tonight with your *friends*."

"I wondered how long it would take before you flung Folly into my teeth."

"It is you who brought up Mr. Ffolliot's name, sir, not I."

"I would try to defend the poor fellow to you, but I doubt it would do a damned bit of good. And I am not about to try to justify my friendship with the man."

"No one asked you to!" Goaded beyond endurance,

it was all Kate could do to keep up the semblance of waltzing. "I am sure I do not care if you choose to sully your good name by associating with such unworthy companions who—who encourage you to play so deep you lose your best horses and—"

"What!" Harry missed a step and another couple nearly crashed into them. His eyes blazed so strangely that she was nigh afraid to speak, but she continued valiantly, "It—it is well known how you had to sell your hunters to meet your gambling debts."

"It is indeed? By whom? Who told you such a thing?"

"Well, I—I . . ." Kate hesitated. Beneath the roilings of Harry's anger, she detected a flash of pain, but not a trace of guilt. And Harry was not the sort of man to dissemble. Kate suddenly felt no longer so sure of herself.

"Never mind. It scarce matters who," Harry said in flat tones. "The important thing is that *you* believed it."

He lapsed into a stony silence, but beneath the grim facade, Kate caught hintings of a deep and abiding hurt. She had the sinking feeling that she had somehow wronged Harry yet again.

The waltz seemed to drag on forever, the lilting music a mockery of the numbing unhappiness and shame Kate felt seeping through her. When the dance ended, Harry no longer looked angry, merely tired, a soul deep weariness dulling his eyes.

"I will escort you back to your grandmother," he said.

"My lord . . ." She trailed off. Now scarce was the time to be asking him for explanations that she should have sought much sooner instead of being so quick to credit Julia's tale.

He offered her his arm, stiff and unyielding. She rested her fingertips against the crook, feeling the distance widen between them as though they had been separated by miles.

To add to Kate's misery, they had not taken many steps when they were accosted by the squire. He greeted Harry in his usual bluff fashion, and what must the wretched fellow do but go nattering on about what a magnificent run he had enjoyed that morning on Harry's own hunter.

Harry tried for an expression of polite indifference but could not quite manage it.

The squire clapped him on the shoulder. "No need to look so glum, sir. I paid you a handsome price for those horses and from what I have heard tell, you are putting the money to good use. What you invest on your lands you will get back tenfold, to say nothing of making the Hudderstons happy as mudlarks."

Kate felt her heart nigh go still. "The Hudderstons?" she asked hoarsely.

The squire chuckled. "Aye, his lordship's tenants these days are likely to dub him 'Saint Harry.'"

"What a parcel of nonsense," Harry said, appearing both annoyed and embarrassed. He tugged at Kate's arm. "If you will excuse us, Mr. Gresham—"

"The lad has been dropping a great deal of his blunt," the squire continued, ignoring Harry. "Fixing up the Hudderston's roof and new drains for the old Stratton place . . ."

Kate closed her eyes, the full impact of exactly how wrong she'd been striking her like a thunderclap. Dear God! Not gaming debts. Harry had used the money to fix up his tenant's farms, those self-same tenants she had accused him of neglecting.

The squire rattled on, warming to his subject with great relish until Harry interrupted him. "I don't think Miss Towers is much interested in roofs and drains."

"Isn't she?" The squire peered fiercely at Kate

from beneath his bushy brows. "Why, I think you mistake her, my lord. I've always said Miss Kate was a cut above these other mutton-headed females. A most sensible girl."

"Indeed I am not," Kate whispered. "I am the greatest of fools."

Neither of the men seemed to hear her as the music struck up again. The squire declared he must seek out Mrs. Gresham for the next dance. "After all these years, I am still her favorite beau." Giving a broad wink, the burly man moved off in search of his wife.

Without his looming presence, Kate felt as though she had been left entirely alone with Harry. She scarce knew how to face him or what to say. Harry gently disengaged his arm from hers.

"I believe Lieutenant Porter is coming to claim you, Miss Towers. So I will simply bid you good night."

"Harry," she faltered, but by the time she could bring herself to look up, Harry was already gone. She caught a glimpse of him disappearing beneath the archway.

The genial lieutenant was doomed once more to be left without a partner, for Kate plunged after Harry. She paused in the hall's open doorway, the cool night air striking against her heated cheeks. Her heart torn with remorse, Kate watched Harry head for the nearby inn yard. In another moment, he would vanish into the night.

Kate hesitated, biting down hard upon her lip. Bishop's daughters did not race in pursuit of young men beneath the light of the moon. But she simply couldn't allow Harry to leave this way. Hitching up her skirts, she started after him.

Harry cleared the ground with long swift strides, obliging Kate to run to catch up with him. Breathlessly, she planted herself in his path.

"H-harry. Please . . . do wait."

Moonlight sculpted his features, throwing the strong hard lines of his profile into sharp relief. His eyes registered neither welcome nor censure, only emptiness.

"Go back, Kate," he said dully. "You should not be out here alone with me. Think of your reputation."

Tears gathered at the ends of Kate's lashes. She drew an unsteady breath. "The—the devil with my reputation!"

At least her vehemence produced some reaction, his brows arching upward in astonishment. She laid one hand against his chest as though that light gesture could somehow stay him.

"I—I am sorry," she said. "I didn't mean to hurt you, to . . . to ever believe— 'Tis only when I heard about the sale of your horses I could not imagine—"

"That there could be any good reason for my actions." Harry finished for her. He looked away, his jaw working painfully. "Damn it, Kate. I am well accustomed to the world cheerfully believing the worst of me, but you! When you join them, it tears me to flinders."

Kate's heart constricted, and she was possessed of a reckless impulse to do anything to make him amends, banish the pain she heard threading his voice. Fully realizing it was not the wisest thing to do, she stood on tiptoe and brushed a kiss along his cheek.

"I am sorry," she whispered again.

It was as though she had set a match to tinder. With a low groan, Harry caught her hard against him, burying his face against the pulse beat at her throat. Kate knew she should protest, but somehow her arms wound about his neck and she clung to him.

But moments before Harry had nearly given in to

despair. When Kate had leveled her false accusation, so full of righteous indignation, he had heard the old bishop speaking. Harry's quest to win her seemed impossible. She would ever be her papa's daughter.

Yet no trace of that prim creature now remained in the woman who so tenderly sought his pardon, the warmth of her arms the gentlest of consolation. Harry meant to do no more than hold her, but the longings of the past two years proved too much for him. The scent of her, the feel of her, all the softness, the sweetness that was Kate drove him nigh to madness.

He began to trail fire-ridden kisses along the column of her neck, the delicate curve of her jaw, her temple, her eyelids. Even if she had resisted, Harry was not sure he could have stopped. But she did not resist, tipping up her face like a rose seeking the warmth of the sun.

"Kate . . . Kate," he murmured between kisses. "I can scarce be patient any longer. *Will* you marry me?"

"I don't know. Oh, I don't know. I feel so . . . confused."

Harry sought to add to that confusion by claiming her lips. He kissed her without mercy, ruthlessly plundering her mouth until she sagged weakly against him.

Papa had warned her, Kate thought muzzily, about the dangers of moonlight and a man like Harry. And Papa had been so right. She shivered with the delicious fiery sensations coursing through her. Caught between despair and rapture, she held Harry tighter, her lips pleading for more.

It was left to Harry to be the one first coming to his senses. Just as his own passion threatened to burst the bounds of reason, he caught the sound of some drunken revelers staggering down the steps of the nearby inn.

In another few moments, he and Kate would be discovered at their moonlight tryst. "The devil with it," Harry thought, bending over her for another kiss, an evil voice seeming to whisper in his ear, that if they were caught in a compromising situation, Kate would have to marry him.

But he did not want her that way, anymore than he wanted her coming to him out of some misguided notion of duty. With a heavy sigh, he summoned up all his willpower and thrust her from him.

She looked momentarily dazed, then hurt and bewildered. Even within the shadows of darkness, he could see the blush that heated her cheeks. Harry forced a smile, speaking in mock sternness.

"This behavior would be outrageous, Miss Towers, even if we were betrothed. You might be ready to consign your reputation to perdition, but I have turned respectable."

Kate gave an indignant gasp, then one of those unwilling gurgles of laughter that so delighted Harry. He took her by the arm, nudging her back toward the hall.

"For I would as soon not exchange greetings with any of those gentlemen heading toward the stables. And I mistake not, they have already shot the cat."

"No! Truly, Harry?" Kate glanced back with a look of horror.

" 'Tis only an expression, sweetheart. It means they are quite inebriated."

"Oh," Kate said with such an innocent relief Harry longed to kiss her all over again. He paused at the steps leading into the assembly hall, hating to take her back inside after all that just passed between them, so much left unsaid.

Kate seemed to feel a reluctance, too, for she

rested her hand timidly upon his sleeve. "Harry . . ." She gazed up at him, her violet eyes earnest and troubled. "I have been so unfair to you."

"Nay, Kate. No more apologies—"

"I do not mean just about the horses," she went on quickly. "But also about what I said awhile ago when you asked me to marry you. *I don't know.* Such a foolish answer."

"On the contrary, it was a most delightful answer." He caught her hand, kissing her fingertips but only lightly, playfully lest he once more be carried away. "You give a fellow cause to hope."

Her lashes fluttered down as though she could not meet his gaze. "I thought I had made up my mind, that I knew what I must do when I came here this evening—"

"If you go near Adolphus Thorpe again other than to hear a sermon—" Harry started to growl.

"I won't," Kate promised with a gentle laugh. "I know that I could never marry him *now.*"

"Kate!" Harry nigh forgot everything, starting to pull her toward him again. But a more formidable threat than the drunkards hove into view. He could see Julia making her way toward the open doorway.

"Damn!" Harry swore.

"It is just as well." Kate said. "I need time to reflect, and I have more than a few words to say to Miss Thorpe."

The fierceness of Kate's expression as she took the stairs and marched back into the hall left Harry gaping with astonishment. If she had been a man, Harry thought he would be offering to be her second. Although he had no clear idea of her quarrel with Julia, he hastened after Kate, intrigued to hear what she would say.

But he was doomed to disappointment. He had not got far when he was cornered by Lady Dane.

"Well?" she demanded.

Harry regarded her questioningly in turn, widening his eyes to the fullest extent of innocence. "Well what, my lady?"

"Do not be pert with me, sir. You have had my granddaughter outside beneath the moon long enough, you had best be prepared to give me tidings of your engagement."

Harry grimaced. He might have known nothing would escape her ladyship's eagle eyes.

"Alas, I have no good tidings to give you as yet. But soon, I feel, very soon." He could not refrain from looking a little smug, remembering Kate's response to his kiss. "And I must tell your ladyship, I find that my methods are far more effective than yours."

"Wicked rogue!" Lady Dane gave him a sharp dig with her cane, but she was smiling.

Harry turned to look for Kate, but to his disappointment, she had already finished with Julia. Kate was taking her place opposite some callow youth for the next dance. She looked as proper as ever, but the color yet glowed high in her cheeks.

A wry smile escaped Harry. She had not accepted his proposal yet, but this time she had not refused him either. Decidedly this was progress. It put him in such a cheerful frame of mind that he was able to watch with equanimity Kate make her way through a succession of dancing partners.

While Lieutenant Porter at last had his dance with her, Harry made his way toward the punch bowl, nearly walking into the Reverend Thorpe.

Adolphus flattened himself against the wall in an effort to stay out of Harry's path. "M-my lord, I beg your pardon."

"Cousin Harry," Harry gently chided him, then walked on, leaving the poor man thoroughly dumbfounded and bewildered.

As Harry sipped his punch, he was astonished to

discover that more than one of his neighboring land-owners had remarked on the improvements he had begun making upon his estates. He found himself the center of a great deal of attention and approval, which rendered him somewhat uncomfortable. He was not at all accustomed to being lauded for virtuous behavior.

"Mapleshade has always been a grand estate," Squire Gresham remarked. "I'd stake it against any other in England."

The other men chorused hearty agreement.

"Perhaps Mapleshade once was worthy of such praise." A chill female voice cut through the masculine ones. Harry glanced down to find Julia unexpectedly at his side. Her disposition was as soured as if she had been drinking lemonade instead of punch. What had Kate said to her? Harry would have given the last of his horses to know.

She continued with a sneer, "There certainly were times far more glorious at Mapleshade than the present. The harvests were much more prosperous, the old fête day the event of the season."

"Ah, well, I am not quite as old as you, Julia," Harry drawled. "I don't remember any of that."

As the men chuckled, Julia turned quite red. "Nor does anyone else. Most of Mapleshade's revered and time-honored customs appear to have ended with your father."

Harry knew he should let this spiteful remark go unchallenged. But damn, it was a jab at the governor as well as himself.

"It so happens," he announced loftily. "That I have every intention of reviving the old fête day."

His statement produced a hubbub of excitement and the squire fairly wrung his hand by way of congratulations. The news spread round the room, and Kate regarded him through eyes glowing with pride.

Harry could not resist raising his punch cup in a

mocking salute to his discomfitted cousin. That was one in the eye for Julia. It was not until he downed the sticky sweet liquid that a daunting thought hit him, nigh causing him to choke.

Harry did not have the damnedest notion what the ancient fête day was.

Chapter 9

What on earth had he done? Harry thought the following morning as he lay flat on his back, staring up at the canopy of the bed looming above him. He could scarce believe he had permitted Julia to goad him into such an undertaking—a revival of the old harvest fête. Great heavens, what did he know about playing lord of the manor?

As he reviewed that disastrous moment at the assembly, when he had grandly made his announcement, he still didn't know what had come over him. He couldn't blame it upon that watery punch. Perhaps it had been the far more heady draught of Kate's sweet eyes trained upon him, so expectant. How could he have disappointed her?

And, he admitted as he stretched, locking his arms behind his head, it had been worth it, the way her face had suffused with delight, her glow of pride in him. He had always wondered why those dashed fool knights had rigged themselves out in all that armor, letting some other dolt take a run at them with a lance, risking being knocked head over ears. Such recklessness could only have been inspired by a lady.

Tilting, however, seemed a plagued sight easier than what he had undertaken. Upon his return home last night, he had asked Gravshaw exactly what the deuce was supposed to take place at this fête. The elderly retainer had explained the holiday had always taken place after the harvest, consisting of a dinner for the laborers, the tenants and the local gentry, to say nothing of the games and the ball held early in the evening. Harry had far rather Gravshaw *had* said nothing of those.

Harry didn't have the damnedest notion of how to arrange any sort of ball or games, at least not respectable ones. And he was not such a mutton head as to believe Sybil was going to be the least use to him. The event was going to turn out an utter shambles. He would undoubtedly make a fool of himself before most of the countryside. Worse still, he would diminish himself in Kate's eyes just as she was nigh ready to fall into his arms.

With a low groan, Harry rolled over when he heard a discreet knock at the door. He barked a curt command to enter and within moments, Gravshaw stood framed in the bedcurtain openings.

"My lord, Lady Dane is belowstairs," the butler began in long suffering accents, "and she—"

"I am just rising." Harry sat bolt upright in alarm, groping for the sheet. "Tell her ladyship I shall be belowstairs directly!"

"Very good, my lord."

Harry could not quite be certain, but he thought his redoubtable manservant heaved a sigh of relief as he quit the room. Fully acquainted with her ladyship's impatience and her methods, Harry wasted no time in repairing to his dressing room.

He shaved and garbed himself in haste, which in nowise disconcerted his valet. Bardle, by this time, was quite used to the young master's fits and starts. Harry was never as inclined to linger over his toilet as that dapper little man would have liked.

As Harry descended the front hall stairs two at a time, he wondered what brought her ladyship down upon him this time. Of all those present at the assembly, he believed that only she had sensed the unease beneath his smiling good humor after he had promised to revive the fête. She had probably come to tell him what an idiot he was, Harry thought with a wry grin. Her ladyship was most adept at that.

He discovered that Gravshaw had escorted her ladyship into the main salon, the most elaborate and formal in the house, well suited to Lady Dane, but not much favored by Harry. The massive chamber was too dark and solemn by half with the furniture done in mahogany, the marble fireplace overly ostentatious, and the draperies a most regal but forbidding gold-fringed purple.

As Harry entered the drawing room, he found her ladyship settled upon a heavily carved chair, and greatly to his astonishment on the settee opposite was Sybil. Not only fully dressed, but belowstairs before two of the clock. For once she was not reclining, but sitting erect like a schoolgirl in the presence of a stern governess, an expression of the most civil terror upon her plump features. Her smelling salts were at her elbow, but she appeared half-afraid to reach for them under Lady Dane's disapproving stare.

"There you are at last, Lytton," her ladyship said before he could so much as bow over her hand. "I have just been informing your stepmama of your plans to hold the harvest day fête."

"You must be quite mad, Harcourt." Sybil sneaked a quick sniff of her salts. "My precarious health will never permit—"

"I am fully aware of the delicate state of your health, madam." Lady Dane's obvious contempt reduced Sybil to quaking silence. "That is why we have ridden over this morning to offer you and Lord Lytton our help."

"We?" Harry asked.

Lady Dane nodded toward someone behind him, a quiet presence who had escaped his notice. Harry turned toward the tall windows, the morning light pouring through them dispelling the chamber's gloom.

But to Harry it was not the sun that accomplished this feat so much as the slight figure who stood outlined by its rays, a vision all soft muslin, lace, and ribbons of rose, her dark hair cascading from beneath a demure straw bonnet.

"Kate," Harry breathed.

When she gave him that half-shy smile, he suddenly felt as though he could conquer a dozen harvest fêtes. Aye, and half the world as well.

Grandmama had presented her suggestion to Kate earlier that morning with her customary delicacy. Sybil Arundel had wool for brains, she said roundly, and Lord Harry was a mere man. Between the two of them, there was no hope that the fête could be a success until some more competent female took a hand. It was the only neighborly and *Christian* thing to do.

It sounded to Kate like a rather shocking piece of interference, but before she quite knew where she was at, she was hustled into her grandmother's carriage and on the way to Mapleshade.

The sight of Harry's genuine relief and gratitude at the offer served to end most of Kate's qualms. After the injustice she had done him, she was eager to join Lady Dane in coming to his aid. But in the busy days that ensued, Kate soon discovered Lady Dane gave the term "we" its most royal usage. Her ladyship's notion of helping was to preside over tea in the parlor while commanding Kate and Harry 'not to dawdle.'

As the Dowager Countess of Lytton took to her bed with a hastily acquired bout of influenza, Kate was obliged to take charge of the proceedings, Harry's household staff coming to her more and more for their instructions regarding the preparations.

Not that Kate actually minded. She had not been so happily occupied since the days she had played hostess for her father at the episcopal palace. She threw herself into the planning with a will, determined to arrange a fête that would do Harry credit and silence forever Julia Thorpe's criticisms of him.

The only aspect of it all that disturbed Kate was that Grandmama was astonishingly lax in her chaperonage, frequently leaving Kate alone in Harry's company. Of course Harry was supposed to be hard at work in his own study, but that room conveniently adjoined the Hunt parlor, which had been assigned to Kate for her use.

More oft than not Harry lounged in the doorway, his gaze warmer than the fire crackling on the hearth to dispel the early autumn chill. Kate tried to concentrate on such weighty matters as the menu for the fête that Harry's cook had submitted for her approval. But it was difficult to ignore that much masculinity leaning against one's door jamb, the sleeves of Harry's linen shirt rolled up to expose the strength of his bronzed forearms.

"Shall I put another log on the fire?" he asked. "Are you quite warm enough, Kate?"

"Yes, my lord."

"If you want anything, you know you have but to say so."

"Yes, my lord."

The rogue-green eyes became more bold, the deep voice soft and suggestive. "We could simply forget all this fête nonsense and you could elope with me today."

"*No*, my lord."

Harry grinned, preparing to retreat. Kate who had been wishing him to leave her in peace, suddenly discovered she could not bear for him to do so.

"No, Harry. Wait . . ."

He paused questioningly.

"I—I do need you."

He beamed, taking an eager step forward.

"To—to help me go over the list of names for the invitations."

Harry came to an abrupt halt, his expectant expression fading to a rueful disappointment. But he straightened his waistcoat, rolling his sleeves down into a more decorous attitude. "I am entirely at your disposal, my lady."

The Hunt parlor boasted at least a half dozen of fine Hepplewhite chairs upholstered in striped silk, the legs and arms finely carved by the hand of a master craftsman. Yet it did not surprise Kate in the least that Harry ignored all those elegant creations and settled beside her on the sofa.

She stiffened with immediate wariness. Harry had behaved like a gentleman since that night of the assembly, but Kate oft detected a most disquieting gleam in his eye. She was not sure she entirely trusted him. Even less did she trust the propriety of her own response. The memory of his kisses had the power to fire her blood, urging her to fling sanity to the winds as she had in the dark shadows of the inn yard.

Feeling a quiver run through her at his nearness, Kate moved further into the corner of the sofa. She reached briskly for the quill pen upon the small writing desk set before her.

"Naturally," she said, "all of your laborers and tenants will attend the fête. But you must decide which of your neighbors you mean to have."

Harry edged closer, ostensibly to peer over her shoulder at the list she was compiling, his dark head drawing alarmingly nigh her own.

"Of course, the Greshams and the Thorpes will be invited." Kate heard her own voice rise a shade higher. "And your stepmama asked me to be sure Mr. Crosbie's name is included."

She felt Harry freeze. Although he moved not a muscle, she sensed the tension that coursed through him.

"Completely out of the question," he said harshly.

Kate glanced up, astonished at the forbidding expression darkening the countenance that had been smiling only a moment before.

"But—but what shall I say to Lady Lytton?" Kate asked.

"I shall deal with her. She should have known better than to suggest such a thing to you. Sybil is well aware how I feel about Mr. Crosbie. He is either a fortune hunter or a fool, I care not which. I won't have him hanging about my stepmother. My father left me the responsibility of looking after her, and that is exactly what I intend to do."

Harry snatched the quill from Kate and scratched out Crosbie's name with such energy, he nigh tore the parchment. Noting the hard determination in Harry's face, Kate did not even think of challenging him upon Lady Lytton's behalf. If Mr. Crosbie was indeed that bad, then she believed Harry's feelings did him credit. But it did rather astonish her to see that he could look as stern as her own papa ever had.

Harry relaxed again as Kate moved on down the list. "The Porters, the Truetts." He nodded with disinterested approval at this recital of the names of the most prominent families in the shire.

When Kate had come to the end, she said, "Is there no one whom I have left off—some particular friend you would wish invited?"

Even as she asked, Kate caught herself hesitating, the memory of Mr. Ffolliot not far from her mind, although both she and Harry, as though by mutual agreement, had ever refrained from mentioning that gentleman's name.

Harry shrugged. "I have complete faith in your judgment, Kate. Ask whomever you think proper."

Kate knew she should not accept this carte blanche, but could not help feeling a little relieved. Harry had a perfect right to receive Mr. Ffolliot if he chose, yet Kate did not know if she could have endured that disreputable man's presence.

She had been focusing so hard upon the list, she did not realize that Harry had stolen the opportunity to inch closer. She started, becoming aware that his arm rested behind her along the sofa, those strong tanned fingers dangling tantalizingly near her shoulder.

Kate trembled at the temptation. She knew she would have to but lean back and offer her lips for him to—

Quickly she shot to her feet. "I had better ring for Gravshaw. He will best be able to help us with planning the dining arrangements."

She half-feared Harry might tug her back down beside him, but she managed to dart trembling round the desk and cross the room in safety. She tugged vigorously at the bellpull.

When she dared glance at Harry, she saw that he had not made one move to intercept her, his eyes glimmering with amusement and impatience.

"Very well. Have it your own way, Miss Towers. But once we have done with this wretched fête, I assure you it will take far more than a butler to come to your rescue."

The threat sounded only part in jest, but Kate could scarce blame Harry for coming to the end of his forebearance. She had been much more fair to him when she had flatly told him no, kept him at a distance.

Her current state of indecision and confusion filled

her with shame. She could scarce deny any longer that she loved Harry, not even to herself. Then what kept holding her back? But one thing—the whisper of a memory. Her father. She could still hear the bishop's voice warning her to proceed with care.

By the time Gravshaw answered her summons, Kate managed to recover her composure. But she avoided the sofa, settling herself primly upon one of the Hepplewhite chairs. Looking rather disgruntled, Harry crossed his arms over his chest. Stretching out his long legs, he propped his boots upon the writing desk, evincing little interest in the arrangements being made for his guests.

Gravshaw however entered into the discussion with all the earnest consideration it deserved. Tables would be set up in the fields for the farmhands, a tent provided for the tenants, while the more distinguished guests would be entertained in the hall's magnificent dining room. The difficulty arose with classifying certain individuals such as the Strattons. Although simple farmers the same as the Hudderstons, Mrs. Stratton now kept a carriage and sent her daughter to an exclusive boarding school.

"If you'll pardon my saying so, Miss Towers," Gravshaw remarked. "Mrs. Stratton is getting above herself. There will be a great deal of resentment if she is raised above her neighbors to the honor of dining room."

"That is very true." Kate frowned, thoughtfully whisking the end of the quill against her chin. And she wanted no such bustle created. Harry's fête must be perfect, without even the shading of any ill will or spiteful gossip to spoil it.

She and Gravshaw continued to fret and speculate for several moments more upon the fate of the annoying Mrs. Stratton until Harry broke in, "For heaven's sake, I don't think Wellington gave such consideration to the deployment of his troops at Waterloo. Let everyone fill their plates and sit where they find room. I am sure I shouldn't complain even if I end up next to old Timothy Keegan."

Kate exchanged a pained look with Gravshaw. Harry, bearing so little regard for his own consequence, could not be expected to understand how those of lesser rank might be far more jealous of theirs. Sighing, Kate gently removed Harry's feet from the desk and suggested he might want to consult with Mr. Warburton to see how the construction of the marquee was coming.

"Trying to be rid of me, eh?" Harry chuckled. "What reward will I receive for taking myself off like a good boy?"

Ignoring this pointed question, Kate took him by the arm and escorted him firmly to the door. "And do make sure Mr. Warburton remembers that we require another tent for the ladies to take tea."

Harry went without resisting, but at the threshold he paused to murmur, "I would gladly do all that you require, Kate, for one kiss."

"For one box on the ears, sir." She thrust him out, but Harry still managed to whisper several more wicked suggestions before she closed the door in his face.

Kate fought down a blush before turning to face Gravshaw, dreading lest he had noticed some of this byplay. She thought she detected a hint of a smile, but by the time she resumed her seat, the elderly butler had settled his face into lines of nigh painful gravity.

Without further interruption from Harry, they were able to settle the matter of seating before teatime, the socially ambitious Mrs. Stratton firmly relegated to the tent where she belonged.

"The cards of invitation have arrived from the printers," Gravshaw said. "Shall I have them brought in?"

"Yes, but you need not rush." Kate pushed back from the desk, flexing her toes within her soft kid boots. "I am rather stiff from sitting so long and should like to take a turn about the garden."

"Very good, my lady." Gravshaw bowed himself out.

It was not until the door had closed behind him that the import of what the dignified manservant had said struck Kate.

My lady.

Kate pressed her hands to her cheeks in dismay. Whether it had been a slip of the tongue or the title used with deliberation scarce mattered. Either prospect was equally disconcerting. Her constant presence at Mapleshade had obviously given rise to expectations, even in the servant's quarters.

But were they expectations she intended to fulfill? Most earnestly did Kate seek to probe the depths of her own heart. What answer would she give the next time Harry asked her to marry him, *seriously* asked?

She had to acknowledge how comfortable she had become these past days, even in her temporary role as mistress of Mapleshade. And its earl ... how much more so dependent upon his presence for her happiness. Odd how the sharing of such simple domestic routines like teatime, dinner, working together on the details of the fête had drawn them into a greater intimacy than ever before. She had observed firsthand how hard Harry strove to be a good master, that combination of humor and firmness with which he treated his dependents.

"He's so different, Papa," Kate murmured, "so different from the wild heedless young man you believed him to be."

If only her father were there to realize it. If only the bishop were there to give his blessing ...

The thought brought with it a wave of melancholy. Kate did her best to shake it off. There was no sense repining for what could never be. The decision regarding Harry was as ever hers to make. Instead of moping here, she would do far better to go for her walk as she had planned. Perhaps the brisk air would clarify her thinking.

Scooping up her shawl, Kate let herself out through one of the French doors leading to Mapleshade's formal garden. She felt glad of the warm wool draped about her shoulders, the nip of September in the air, despite the sun glinting along the gravel pathways.

Most of the flowers had lost their bloom, the roses dying on the vine, yet Kate still reveled in the orderly layout of the beds, the neat rows of hedges all a delight to her tidy soul. She filled her lungs with the crisp air and wandered toward the summerhouse, a pagodalike structure that stood at the hub of the garden.

She had no intention of going inside, merely skirting past it. But her plans were abruptly altered when an arm shot out of the shadowy depths and yanked her beneath the arched opening.

Kate let out a squeak of surprise. She could not imagine that it would be other than Harry perpetrating such mischief. It was on the tip of her tongue to scold him for giving her such a fright, when her gaze adjusted to the pagoda's gloom-filled interior. It was not Harry's green eyes that twinkled back at her, but those of a stranger, looking rather nervous and frightened himself.

His cherubic features framed by ridiculously high starched shirt points, the young man appeared harmless enough, but he did not relax his grasp upon her wrist.

Kate's lips parted to cry out.

"Oh, don't scream," a female voice shuddered. " 'Twill go right through my head."

Kate's mouth closed. She glanced down with astonishment to discover Lady Lytton seated on a bench. Apparently she had made a remarkable recovery from her influenza. Despite the chill of the day, her gown sported a shockingly low decolletage. The gooseflesh forming beneath the dusting of pearl powder made an interesting effect, and the glow in her ladyship's cheeks for once owed to more than rouge.

"We didn't mean to alarm you, Miss Towers." The strange young man said. " 'Tis only that we saw you passing by and could not allow such an opportunity for seeing you alone to escape us."

Lady Lytton beamed at him as though he had said something remarkably clever. "Indeed, Miss Towers. I was most desirous to have you make this gentleman's acquaintance. This is Mr. Lucillus Crosbie."

"Mr. Crosbie!" Kate gasped. She wrenched her hand away as though he had suddenly become a snake banding her wrist. *The* Lucillus Crosbie? The same one she had heard Harry denounce with such vehemence only an hour before? Kate backed nervously toward the arched opening.

"Indeed, sir. You should not be here—"

"Of course, he shouldn't," Lady Lytton interrupted petulantly. "Why do you think we are hiding in here?"

"If Lord Harry discovers you . . ." Kate shuddered to think what Harry might do.

Mr. Crosbie visibly shared her sentiments. He paled, saying, "His lordship tossed me out twice, once into the pond, once out the window."

"Did he?" Kate's alarm grew, having no desire to witness Harry inspired to such violence. "Then I think your wisest course would be to leave at once, sir."

"But we must talk to you," her ladyship wailed.

"It will do no good. I already told Lord Harry

about your wish that Mr. Crosbie attend the fête and he said—"

"Oh, plague take the fête," Mr. Crosbie exclaimed with great passion. He clasped Lady Lytton's hand to his heart. "Miss Towers, we can bear this separation no longer. We want to be married."

Kate's mouth gaped open and she had to force it closed. Gazing from the pink-cheeked young man to the lady nigh twice his age, she thought she had never been more shocked. She felt much like a swimmer already aware of being in dangerous shallows who suddenly plunges in over her head.

She sagged down onto a bench opposite the duo clutching each other in such dramatic fashion. "I-I doubt Harry will ever permit such a thing."

"I know that." Lady Lytton sniffed, groping for her handkerchief. "He has been behaving like . . . like a regular Capulet."

The image of Harry playing tyrannical parent to Lady Lytton's Juliet was a ludicrous one, but Kate did not feel in the least like laughing. She scarce knew what to say to this pair of ill-assorted lovers, but they apparently mistook her silence for encouragement and began to pour out their hopes and mutual devotion.

"Lord Lytton does not believe I love Sybil, but I do," Mr. Crosbie declared. "He cannot understand. Miss Towers, I have a mama and seven older sisters. Seven! Not a one of them has ever taken my ambition to be a sculptor seriously. They think I should join the army." He paused to direct a speaking glance at her ladyship. "Only Sybil has ever believed in me."

"Dear boy!" She squeezed his hand. "You shall rival Michelangelo."

"I am now in a position to support a wife," Mr. Crosbie continued eagerly. "Thanks to Sybil's patronage, I have obtained some commissions in Chillingsworth to work on some tombs in the cathedral."

Recalling the memorial Mr. Crosbie had designed for Harry, Kate had a horrifying vision of the future decor of that ancient and venerable church, but she managed to say, "My ... my congratulations, Mr. Crosbie, but I do not understand why you chose to confide in me. The proper person to address would be Lord Harry—"

"He will not listen!" Mr. Crosbie said. "At least not to us."

"But to you, my dear—" Lady Sybil began.

"Oh, no. No!" Kate repeated firmly as she realized what they were about to ask her. She started to rise, but this time she was detained by Sybil's plump hand. She angled an arch glance at Mr. Crosbie. "My dear Lucillus, if you could but allow me a moment alone with Miss Towers."

He looked loath to leave her, but he agreed, his eyes so rapt with adoration Kate doubted he would have refused any request of Lady Lytton's. He retreated to the opposite end of the summerhouse, out of earshot.

Kate longed to retreat as well, not sure what was coming next. With her youthful lover gone, Lady Lytton bundled up more sensibly within the folds of her own shawl, abandoning the simper she habitually wore.

"I daresay you think me quite a silly old woman, my dear," she said. Ignoring Kate's mild protest she rushed on, "But I am not so silly I don't know my own mind. I was quite young when I married the first time, Miss Towers. Harry's papa picked me out of the line of debutantes at Almack's in less time than he spent choosing a horse."

She winced. "Such a great booming voice my lord had, but it was a good match. My parents were pleased." Her ladyship's soft chin stiffened with resolution. "This time I am old enough to marry to please myself, and I shall do so. Lucillus is so gentle, so . . . so sensitive. I don't want to cause poor Harcourt any sort of scandal, but he is making me quite desperate."

Lady Lytton angled a coy and coaxing glance at Kate, reaching out to pat her hand. "You could avert much of this discord, Miss Towers. I am not such a widgeon that I haven't noticed the way Harcourt looks at you. You could talk him round."

Kate started to deny she had any such power over Harry, but she could not quite manage to do so. For she feared she could persuade Harry if she set herself to the task, and strangely enough she was not unsympathetic to Lady Lytton's cause. The world might raise its eyebrows at such a peculiar match, but Kate detected a genuine vein of affection running beneath all of her ladyship's and Mr. Crosbie's melodramatic protestations.

But to agree to use her influence with Harry in their behalf, the sort of influence a wife might exert upon a husband, why that was tantamount to confirming the tie between herself and Harry.

Yet Kate was not proof against the entreaty in Lady Lytton's eyes. "I—I suppose I could try," she murmured with great reluctance.

Even this vague promise was enough to set Lady Lytton into transports of delight. She called over Mr. Crosbie and the pair of them nigh overwhelmed Kate with their expressions of gratitude. Kate nodded weakly, inching toward the arch, at last making good her escape. She left them holding hands, whispering tender vows and all manner of wildly impractical plans.

"Whew!" Kate sighed as she all but fled back to the house. She must have taken complete leave of her senses. Whatever had induced her to become involved in Lady Lytton's romantic tangle when Kate could not even manage to sort out her own? She regretted the pledge she had given, but it was not in Kate to go back on her word.

She entered the house with a feeling of trepidation, not looking forward to broaching the subject with Harry. She had never seen him quite so fierce about anything as his loathing for Mr. Crosbie.

To her relief, she was granted a temporary reprieve. Harry had ridden out upon some errands and was not expected back until dinner. After the unsettling interview with Harry's stepmama, it was all Kate could do to seat herself at the desk and commence the mundane task of addressing the invitations.

Her promise to Lady Lytton continued to prey upon her mind even as she dipped her quill into the ink. Perhaps with Harry returning so late, she had best wait until tomorrow to approach him. No, tomorrow was Sunday and on Monday, she recalled, he was engaged to attend a horse auction with the squire and after that— By degrees, Kate convinced herself, it might be best to even wait until after the fête.

If the day was the success she hoped, Harry would like be in a most congenial mood and . . . and . . . Kate paused in midstroke, recollecting that after the fête, Harry had hinted he had strong designs. Might he not likely counter her plea for Lady Lytton with some tender demands of his own? Demands that sent a shiver of anticipation coursing through Kate.

Blushing at her own imaginings, Kate nearly knocked over the inkstand as she heard the parlor door creaking open. Harry? Her defenses immediately went up, she called out, "I am addressing the invitations, my lord. If you have come to torment me, I shall never—"

The half-playful warning died upon her lips as she glanced up. It was not Harry who paused upon the threshold, but Miss Thorpe, the crisp silk of her frock rustling against the frame.

"Oh. Julia," Kate said in flat tones.

Miss Thorpe gave her a brittle smile. Relations between Kate and the vicar's sister had been less than cordial since the eve of the assembly. Kate had not outright accused Julia of lying, but she had made it quite plain she no longer cared to hear anything from Miss Thorpe regarding Harry.

After an awkward pause, Julia said, "I came to call upon Lady Lytton, but when Gravshaw told me you were in here, I could not resist stopping in. I . . . I trust you are not still angry with me over that unfortunate misunderstanding about Lytton?" This last was pronounced in a hesitant manner far different from Julia's usual forthright speech.

"No, I am not angry," Kate said quietly, "but I fear I am rather occupied." She bent over the invitations again, hoping that Julia would take the hint and just go away.

Instead Julia glided further into the room to peer over Kate's shoulder. "Oh, dear, I did not realize Lytton had pressed you into service as his secretary." She essayed a light laugh, but it was obvious her amusement was forced.

"I don't mind in the least," Kate said. Her quill spattered some ink upon one of the vellum cards. She sought to blot it, stifling an impatient exclamation. It was nigh impossible to proceed with Julia hovering at her elbow, reading the guest list, her gloved fingers fidgeting with the stack of invitations.

"You have been so occupied of late. I have missed you, Kathryn," she said. "There is a scarcity of congenial company to be found in this wretched village."

Kate doubted Julia would succeed in finding 'congenial company' wherever she might be, but Miss Thorpe's voice held a threading of real unhappiness. Though she hardly knew why, Kate was moved by a feeling of pity for the beautiful, self-possessed woman.

"I shall have more time to spare after the fête," Kate said.

"Will you? Somehow I doubt that." Julia took a restless turn about the room, a moody expression marring the lovely lines of her profile. "I greatly fear that you will soon have less time for me than ever. One would have to be blind not to see what your constant presence at Mapleshade portends. The entire village is preparing to wish you joy."

Kate supposed she should have been disconcerted by Julia's words. Only days ago, she would have been quick to refute them. But now the phrase seemed to stick in her mind, like a most gentle and beguiling melody. *Wish you joy*—the words conjured up images of church bells and wedding days . . . images of Harry.

A tiny smile curved Kate's lips, soft with all a young girl's dreamings. She had no idea how the expression transformed her features, but Julia noted it—the faraway look that brightened Kate's eyes, the flush that tinted her cheeks.

It was as though Kate hovered on the brink of some great happiness, a happiness and contentment Julia sensed she would never know. She suddenly felt blighted and far older than her twenty-seven years.

Her own plans had turned to ash. Since Lytton's jealous display at the assembly, Adolphus declared he would not go near Kate except to read the service of her marriage to the earl. And Julia's attempts to discredit Lytton had misfired, what with all those fools like the squire fawning over the improvements his lordship was making at Mapleshade.

Even her effort to remind everyone of Lytton's neglect, taunting him over the abandonment of the estate's ancient customs, had proved a dismal failure. Who would have guessed that Lytton would take up the challenge and the reviving of the fête would draw him closer to Kate than ever?

With Kate's help, the fête would be a success. Wasn't that how things had always gone for Lytton? No matter how undeserving he was, her reckless cousin bore a charmed existence, always emerging the winner. But then he was a man, Julia thought with unreasoning anger, able to have whatever he had wanted from life, education, travel, the freedom to do whatever he damned well pleased.

Now Lytton would have the bishop's daughter as well, while Julia remained buried alive to the end of her days in Lytton's Dene with her fool of a brother.

Oh, but Kate would eventually be sorry. Lytton might be a pattern card of behavior now, letting her arrange the fête to her satisfaction, with her proper list of guests, but wait a month or two. The earl's disreputable companions would once more overrun Mapleshade and—

Yet why did it have to take a month or two? A sudden notion caused Julia to suck in her breath, a notion that should never have occurred to a vicar's sister, nor to any other lady.

But Julia Thorpe was a most desperate woman. She half glanced away from Kate, fearing that her guilty intentions must show upon her face, but Kate had gone back to her work with the invitations and was not even looking at Julia.

Concealing her nervousness, Julia sidled toward the desk.

"I suppose I must leave you to your task. If I linger here too long, Adolphus will be wondering where I am. The poor man cannot even order up his own dinner without me."

As she leaned over the writing table to make her farewells, she quickly palmed several of the blank invitation cards and hid them in the folds of her skirts. She held her breath, but Kate did not notice a thing.

Too anxious and relieved to be rid of me, Julia thought with a stab of anger and unexpected hurt. "After all your hard work," she said to Kate with a glinting smile as she let herself out, "I do trust this fête proves a roaring success."

Safely on the other side of the door, she stuffed the stolen cards into her reticule, her mouth pinching with a hard determination.

"Aye, a roaring success," she repeated bitterly. "But not if I can help it."

Chapter 10

The day of the fête, Kate peeked out the cottage door and cast an anxious glance toward the skies. But after a week of intermittent rain, it appeared as though the heavens themselves had decided to cooperate. The deep blue soaring above Kate's head looked as though it had been splashed by a painter's brush, the cottony wisps of clouds placed by an artist's hand. The noontide sun warmed her cheeks, promising one of those delicious days when summer seemed to have strayed back into the midst of autumn.

A perfect day . . . what could possibly go wrong? Unfortunately Kate could think of nigh half a dozen things. The chef could burn the sauce for the ducklings, the fiddlers for the dance could forget to come, the fieldhands could consume too much ale and begin a drunken brawl, Lady Lytton could take to her bed with a megrim and not even be there to act as Harry's hostess.

Kate fretted her lip, wishing she could be at his side. But that would have been improper in the extreme, giving rise to even more gossip. All she could do was to take her place among the guests, attempt to smile, while inwardly she would be on pins and needles of apprehension.

Kate had to content herself with arriving at Mapleshade as early as possible. With this view in mind, she ducked back into the house to urge her mother and grandmother to make haste.

Despite the warmth of the day, Kate insisted upon seeing her mother bundled into a woolen shawl.

"I am not a hothouse flower," Mrs. Towers protested, then gave a gentle laugh when Kate foisted a parasol upon her as well to keep off the sun.

"You are not used to being so much out of doors, Mama," Kate said. "But if it becomes too much for you, I daresay you can rest in one of the parlors." She gave her mother's hand a reassuring squeeze. "And you need not fret about the company. I know you are shy of greeting a parcel of strangers. But you are acquainted with the squire's wife and, with his lordship's permission, I invited some of the people from Chillingsworth. Your friend Mrs. Prangle and her daughters will be present."

Mrs. Towers winced and for a moment looked so ill, Kate feared that Mama might not be able to attend after all. But she recovered herself and thanked Kate in a tremulous voice.

Suffused with a warm glow of having done her mother a tremendous kindness, Kate bustled off to see what was keeping Lady Dane. But her ladyship was not to be hurried.

She declared, "I have never been so vulgar as to arrive first at any function, and I do not intend to begin at this time of my life."

There was naught Kate could do for the next half hour but pace the front hall in frustration, alternately straightening the brim of her straw hat with its flowing ribbons, and smoothing the folds of her lavender gown, the starch in her white lace tucker already going a little limp.

It was past one of the clock when they finally left the house and mounted into Lady Dane's regal carriage. Kate was in a fever of impatience by the time the coach straggled through the park gates, lumbering down the sweeping drive that led to Mapleshade.

The sun glowed warm off the hall's red brick, the wings of the magnificent old house seeming to extend like welcoming arms. Kate drew some comfort from the fact that others appeared to be fashionably late as well. She could just see the Prangles vanishing into the house to make their curtsies to their host, while liveried footmen in their tricornes sprang to assist the Gresham family from their carriage.

Being nearest to the door, Kate was the first of her own party to alight. As she turned to make certain Mama descended in safety with the footman's aid, Kate caught sight of a startling apparation. An urchin darted past, so small he was not yet in breeches, his stubby legs protruding from beneath his frock. The child's head was all but lost beneath a man's high-crowned beaver hat, the brim of which sagged over his pudgy nose.

Yet somehow the lad found his way across the drive to where a group of other children were shrieking and gleefully clambering over the massive stone lions that graced the forecourt, their fierce dignity somewhat diminished by being ridden like donkeys.

Kate had no difficulty recognizing the sandy-colored hair and freckles of the numerous Hudderston progeny. She gave a soft exclamation of surprise as she had no difficulty recognizing the tall figure in their midst either.

There was no need for any of the guests to hasten within to greet their host, Kate thought wryly, for the lord of the manor stood at this moment, laughingly scooping up the same imp who had purloined his hat.

The dark strands of his hair tumbled appealingly across his brow; Harry whirled the small boy in a circle, heeding neither possible damage to his immaculate bisquit-colored breeches or the sapphire blue frock coat straining across his shoulders. His glossy black beaver hat flew from the child's head, spinning across the lawn.

"Harry," Kate murmured ruefully. She stalked toward him, retrieving the hat and brushing its brim. But how did one begin to scold a man bringing such happiness to a chubby-cheeked babe, the little one's shrill giggles blending with the deep boom of Harry's own laughter.

"My lord," she began severely.

"Kate!" Harry set the child down at once. His eyes warmed at the sight of her. "Little deserter! There you are at last. How dare you leave me so long at the mercy of these hoards of descending brigands."

The children shrieked with delight at this description, immediately beginning to brandish all sorts of imaginary weapons.

"This—this is scarcely a proper way to greet your guests," Kate said, her voice unsteadied by an unwilling ripple of amusement.

"Indeed it is not." His voice dropped to a husky murmur. "But if I greeted you the way I think I should, your grandmama would whack me with her cane."

Harry captured Kate's hand and raised it to his lips, the warmth of his mouth caressing her fingertips in such a fashion any lady might be pardoned for dealing him a sharp rap. How could Harry make even a kiss upon the hand so wonderfully improper?

Yet Kate had no thought of rebuking him. Her heart thudded out a reckless beat, but she managed to say, "Th—these children should be shooed around to the back. They might hurt themselves and—"

"Nonsense. I always played upon these lions as a boy. I think the old fellows must have got rather lonely over the years. They should have children romping over them."

Despite herself, Kate was beset by a most appealing image of curly-haired moppets, their ringlets Harry's midnight hue, their eyes, his laughing green.

"Half a dozen at least," she murmured, then realizing what she had said, felt herself flush scarlet to the roots of her hair.

Harry merely smiled. Their eyes met, and a current seemed to rush between them. Harry started to speak, but little could be said with the children all eager ears and yet another coach arriving down the drive.

Sighing, Harry tucked her arm beneath his, and they headed toward the house. As they walked up the stairs, beneath the ivy-twined pillars, Kate was astonished at how familiar it already seemed to her. In a curious way, it was like being a weary traveler who had at last come home.

Harry escorted Kate, her mother, and Lady Dane into Mapleshade's massive dining chamber where Lady Lytton was stationed to receive guests. Besides affording immediate access to the south lawn where the marquee was erected, the room was one of the most magnificent in the manor, a relict of the original house, the walls hung with priceless seventeenth-century tapestries woven in Belgium.

Lady Lytton made an odd contrast, very modern in her Grecian-style gown, banded so high and tight that it plumped her bosom to a most alarming state of fullness. Her cheeks were berouged, her curls as brassy as ever, but she greeted each new arrival graciously enough, only occasionally wincing at voices shrill with merriment.

As Kate made her curtsy, Lady Lytton wrung her hand and cast her a conspiratorial glance that rendered Kate acutely uncomfortable. Under the cover of all the bright chatter, her ladyship managed to whisper, "You still have not spoken to Harcourt?"

"No," Kate murmured. "But I promise I will attempt it today."

"I do hope so, my dear for Lucillus grows quite impatient, and I feel ready to perish with longing myself. If we do not obtain Harcourt's consent soon, we will be forced to do something quite *drastic*."

By this time, Kate was accustomed to her ladyship's dramatic utterances. All the same she felt relieved to move on, surrendering her place to the next arrival. Kate yet doubted the wisdom of attempting to interfere on Lady Lytton's behalf, but she had to admit that, today, if any day, Harry might be approachable.

He sparkled with more than his customary good humor as he circulated the crowded room, herding people out onto the lawn, with a quick smile here, a bit of banter there.

Harry might be slow to notice a collapsing roof unless his attention was drawn to it, but he seemed to never forgot a name or a face even among the least of his tenants, nor the smallest details of their existence such as who had recently recovered from a bout of ague, or whose child was due to be christened soon.

It was people, not things, that mattered to Harry, and *that*, Kate was rapidly coming to realize, was one of his most endearing traits. Her heart swelling with pride and love, she could scarce tear her gaze from him, her spirits remaining unruffled even when Julia Thorpe entered the room.

She bid good day to the icy blonde with equanimity, although she did half fear Julia would attach herself to her side as usual. Julia, however, seemed uncommonly distracted herself, her eyes turning so often to the door even Squire Gresham was provoked into commenting upon it.

"Hah, Miss Thorpe, what handsome beau are you expecting?"

Kate rather expected Julia to give the poor man a look of chilling disdain, but instead a faint guilty color stole into her cheeks. It was the first time Kate had ever seen Miss Thorpe blush. She wondered if, amazingly enough, the squire's jest might be true, but Julia recovered herself quickly.

"I am merely breathless with anticipation," she drawled. "I have never attended a party given by my cousin before, and Lord Lytton is always so full of surprises."

"I doubt there will be any today," Kate was quick to snap.

"You may be right." Julia shot one more glance at the door, her mouth drawing down into an expression of disgust and disappointment. She turned abruptly and made her way out onto the lawn.

Kate scarce had much time to wonder at Julia's odd behavior, for she soon exited from the dining chamber herself. Mama, she thought, was looking a little lost, so Kate made sure she found Mrs. Prangle. Kate settled her mother upon a bench beneath one of the towering maples and left her to enjoy the company of her old friend.

Of course, Kate had no need to see to Lady Dane's comfort. Lady Dane strolled across the lawn like a visiting dignitary, inspiring young Becky Gresham and the Misses Prangle to curtsy so low, their muslin frocks seemed in imminent peril of grass stains. With the others of her party suitably entertained, it was herself Kate found at a loss.

She paced the grounds anxiously, but Harry's household staff had executed all her careful plans with great efficiency. Two colorful silk tents had been erected upon the lawn, the smaller a place for the ladies to retire out of the heat, the larger set up with baize-covered benches for the tenantry to dine.

Further into the park, tables had been placed for the laborers, along with a stand to hand out ale in decorous amounts. Space had been cleared for the games, with greased poles for climbing, an area marked off for footraces, a dais built for Harry to hand out the prizes, and a circle where pony rides had been arranged for the tenants' children, this last being Harry's notion.

All progressed as smoothly as though Mapleshade had been the sight of such revelry for years. Left with nothing to do, Kate wandered aimlessly toward the part of the lawn where targets had been mounted and bows and arrows provided. Becky Gresham was demonstrating her prowess at archery while flirting with some nattily dressed stripling in a manner that would have quite shocked her mama.

The sun climbed steadily toward the hottest part of the afternoon. Realizing she had forgotten her parasol, Kate prepared to retreat toward the tent when a hand took her by the elbow.

"Come now, Miss Towers," a teasing male voice scolded. "Wilting so soon? You cannot retire until you have had your turn at the targets."

She glanced up to find Harry smiling down at her. "Do allow me to give you a lesson with the bow."

She was more than glad to see him, but she eased away, demurring. "No, my lord. It would not be right. You should see to your guests."

"I have greeted every last one of 'em in the approved lordlike manner. Besides you are one of my guests. You may as well enjoy it, for next year . . ."

He left the threat unfinished, a challenge in his eye. He half expected Kate to poker up as she often did at such hintings, but instead she acquiesced meekly, holding out her hand for the bow.

"Very well, my lord."

Harry's triumph in having achieved his object, being near to Kate, was only mildly diminished by the fact that he knew next to nothing about archery. The sport had always struck him as a little tame, but he managed to string a bow.

Next came the part he liked best, slipping his arms about Kate to help her take aim at the target. She was not in the least stiff, leaning trustingly against him as he arranged his hands over hers, fitting the arrow into place.

"Now take aim." He lowered his face until it was level with hers, the velvety soft curve of her cheek but a breath away, the wisps of her curls tickling his nose, the sweet, fresh scent of her more seductive than any perfume.

Would this accursed day never come to an end? Plague take the fête! He was beset with an urge to whisper to her right now all the things he had been longing to say, fairly confident of her answer.

Barely he restrained himself. No, by God, this time he would do it right. Later when all the guests were gone, and— No, not the Hill this time. That had proved unlucky.

Harry helped Kate draw back the bow while thinking the garden, perhaps. He would even go down upon one knee, forcing his clumsy tongue to find all the right words, and then she would be in his arms, her lips eager. . . .

Kate released the bow, the shot going wild. It was only then Harry realized how flushed she was as she stepped out of the circle of his arms. They both glanced to where her arrow now lodged in the trunk of an ancient oak.

"I am sorry," Harry said. "Don't eat me, Kate. But I have a confession to make. I don't know a blamed thing about archery."

"No, but I do," Kate said softly. "I have done it frequently."

Harry could only stare at her, the reason for her deception as patently obvious as his own. She looked so adorably flustered and sheepish that Harry was on the verge of forgetting his guests and his carefully laid plans for the garden when he heard someone calling his name.

"I say, Lytton! Where the deuce are you?"

The amiable voice sounded damnably familiar, but it could not be. Harry turned slowly, then cursed under his breath at the sight of the slender young man approaching, twirling a cane, his hat tipped to a jaunty angle.

Folly! What the deuce was he doing here? And with Lord Erwin trailing in his wake. Harry's lips thinned at the sight of the peer noted chiefly for his doubtful linen and coarse manners. Erwin's bewhiskered jowls put one in mind of a pugnacious bull dog, the expression in his small, dark eyes equally as mean.

Too confounded to react, Harry stood frozen until Folly spotted him and tripped over, beaming.

"Here we are at last, old boy. I nigh forgot the right turning in the lane," he said, just as though he had been expected all along. Harry began to wonder if he was losing his mind.

Before he could say a word, Folly's face lit up and he swooped down upon Kate. "Ah, Miss Towers, you here? So delighted to see you again."

Kate had blanched, going rigid with shocked disapproval. But Folly, poor ass, would never be likely to notice that. He bowed over Kate's hand as if she were his oldest and dearest friend.

Erwin made not the slightest effort to greet anyone. He stared about him, scowling. "What the devil is all this, Lytton?"

"I was about to ask you the same thing," Harry muttered. "Why have you come?"

Folly, overhearing the question, released Kate's

clenched fingers, his eyes rounding with surprise. "Why, have I got the wrong day again? Nay, I cannot have. It says right here on the invitation." With that he fished a slightly rumpled card from his pocket.

A tiny gasp escaped Kate. Harry was equally confounded. Good lord! Could Kate possibly have invited . . . No, it was obvious she hadn't, for she was looking at Harry with an expression of utter betrayal. Stumbling about, she gathered up her skirts and fled across the lawn.

"Kate!" Harry cried taking a distracted step after her, but he could scarce go haring off until he had sorted to the bottom of this.

"What is amiss with her?" Folly asked.

"Starched-up female," Erwin growled. "Where are the Cyprians?"

"And when is the mill to take place?" Folly chimed in. "Have we missed it?"

"What in blazes are you talking about?" Harry thought he was about to run mad.

"It says it all right here in the postscript of your invitation." Folly waved the vellum before Harry's eyes.

Harry seized it, frowning at the inked lines promising all manner of diversions from a prize fight to "young ladies more than willing to play Hunt the Squirrel." Whoever was responsible for this mischief had done a credible job of imitating Harry's own spatterdash style of handwriting.

"This is someone's notion of a very poor jest," he said, crushing the invitation in his fist.

"We rode out nigh ten miles for a jest?" Erwin snarled.

"No mill?" Folly asked, his mouth drooping with disappointment.

"I am afraid not and as you can see, the entertainment here is not at all the sort you would care for—"

"You mean," Folly interrupted. "you didn't even invite us?"

"You would not like such a party. It is mostly to reward my tenants and laborers—"

"I believe my lord is trying to tell us," Erwin said, his eyes narrowing dangerously, "he intends to order us off his grounds."

"I say! Harry!" Folly protested.

Harry sighed. He did not give a damn for any of Erwin's angry bluster. He had never much liked the man, considering him a deplorable influence on weak-minded fellows like Mr. Ffolliot. Harry found it much more difficult to harden his heart against his old friend. Folly was regarding him with a mixture of hurt and chagrin like a small boy being chased off from joining in a game of cricket.

"Of course you are welcome to stay," Harry conceded. "As long as you remain on your best behavior. My guests here today are the like of the squire, the vicar, clergy from Chillingsworth, elderly ladies. I would not have any of them offended."

"Certainly not!" Folly brightened. "You need not lecture me like I was a dashed schoolboy, Harry."

Harry arched one brow in dubious fashion. He would far rather Folly and Erwin had gone, but saw no remedy for the situation. His immediate concern was to find Kate and clear up this misunderstanding. Although uneasy about leaving the pair to wander tame among his staid guests, Harry excused himself.

Watching Harry go, the honorable Mr. Ffolliot shook his head. "Vicars? Clergy? Elderly ladies? What's got into Harry?"

"Heard tell as how he's been dangling after some parson's daughter." Lord Erwin snorted with disgust. "That's enough to be the ruination of any man. Let's get out of here."

"Nay, don't be so hasty, sir. There's oft jolly sport

to be found at these fête things, usually some sort of games, I believe. We might get up a wager or two."

Erwin mopped his sweating brow with a soiled handkerchief. "I suppose I could use a drop of something to wet my throat. Let's see what's being dished out in that tent over there."

The two men strode toward the smaller of the two tents, ducking beneath the silk flap. The only one about was a young footman arranging dainty silk-cushioned stools next to a table bearing a silver urn.

Pulling a face, Folly gave the tea service a wide berth, moving toward a promising-looking punch bowl. As he bent over, stirring a ladle through the golden-colored liquid, he sniffed suspiciously, catching the odor of lemon.

"Damnation! You—you don't suppose Harry really means for us to drink this stuff?" Folly exclaimed.

"Wouldn't surprise me. The man's become as priggish as a bleedin' Methodist." Erwin's mouth tipped into a sly leer. "Fortunately, I always come prepared."

Waiting until the footman had left, his lordship reached beneath his frock coat and produced a small flask that he uncorked. He sniffed the contents with appreciation.

"Blue Ruin," he announced and proceed to tip the flask, dumping the gin into the lemonade.

"Here now!" Folly said. "I don't think you ought to be doing that, Erwin."

"Why not? If Lytton is too big a nipsqueeze to provide proper refreshment, then his guests must perforce look to themselves."

Raising the ladle, Erwin took a sip. "Still too weak." Before Folly's horrified gaze, he produced a second flask that he also poured into the punch bowl. Folly considered himself a two bottle man, but only the finest Madeira. Gin was—well, damned coarse, fit for naught but the lower orders.

Satisfied with his creation, Erwin was just about to dip himself out a cupful when a stern voice rang out. "Sir! My lord, I beg your pardons."

Folly whipped about as guiltily as if he had been the one plying the gin. Framed in the tent opening, he saw that stiff-necked manservant of Harry's, the butler he believed, name of Gravedigger or some such.

The elderly retainer did not appear to have noticed Erwin's actions for he said with frigid courtesy, "This tent is solely for the use of the ladies, but if you gentlemen would be pleased to follow me, I shall provide you with more suitable refreshments."

For the ladies! Folly stared at Erwin aghast. But his lordship merely shrugged, his mouth splitting into a malicious grin.

It took Harry so long to find Kate, he had begun to fear she had ordered up her carriage and gone home. He located her at last, leaning against the maple near the area where the children were taking their pony rides. She stared at the ground, fidgeting with the handle of her parasol, her face shadowed with unhappiness.

"Kate." Harry hastened to plant himself in front of her. Bracing one hand on either side of her against the tree trunk, he cut off any possibility of escape.

She made no move, expect for her initial start of surprise. Paling, she refused to glance up, the thickness of her lashes veiling her eyes.

"I realize how it must appear to you, Kate," Harry said. "But I would not have invited Folly here, knowing how you feel about him. And certainly I would not have asked a peep of day boy like Erwin."

"They had a card—" she began.

"How they got it, I have no idea. If you didn't send it—"

"Of course, I didn't," she choked.

"Then someone tried to stir up a nasty piece of mischief. I have no notion of whom, but I shall get to the bottom of it before the day is out."

A seemingly endless silence ensued, in which Harry could do naught but regard her anxiously. Then she raised her head, her earnest gaze probing his. Slowly, she nodded. In that moment, Harry felt much like a general, finally emerging the victor in a hard-fought campaign.

She believed him. She trusted him.

He cupped his fingers gently beneath her chin. "Don't worry, Kate," he said. "I won't let them do anything to spoil our fête."

His reassurance coaxed a smile from her. Her lips were so sweet and inviting, he would have given much to linger, steal a kiss, but despite Folly's assurances, the honorable Samuel had a way of creating disasters and Harry didn't trust Erwin one jot. If he was going to keep his pledge, he need must tear himself away from Kate. He did so with reluctance, his only consolation that before this day's end, he would himself wring a pledge from Kate, one that would bind her to him forever.

Even though she watched Harry depart with regret, Kate's spirits soared from the misery that had engulfed her but moments before. It had been a jolt to see Mr. Ffolliot and Lord Erwin arrive. It had not hurt her that Harry had asked them, so much as the thought he had done so without warning her. She had not wanted to believe it, but the invitation card had seemed incontrovertible proof.

She was so very glad to know she had been wrong. For all Harry's faults, deceit was not among them. But who could have played such a terrible trick? Kate's mind drifted back to the day she had been addressing invitations, a sudden clear image of Miss Thorpe leaning over the writing desk.

No, surely not! Kate was shocked by her own suspicion. Despite Julia's unreasoning dislike of Harry, Kate could not picture the vicar's sister doing anything so dishonorable, so . . . so deliberately cruel.

Yet the thought persisted to trouble her. It only added to her distress to perceive that Mama was not having a good time, either. It was the most pernicious thing, but Kate observed that every time Mrs. Prangle settled in for a comfortable prose with Mrs. Towers, along would come Lady Dane. Grandmother's icy hauteur quite cowled the archdeacon's wife and frightened her from Mama's side.

Her poor mother retreated at last into the tent that had been erected for the ladies. Scolding herself for not looking after her mother better, Kate hurried to join her.

A few other women had also retired out of the heat, among them Mrs. Gresham and Julia. Kate longed to ask Miss Thorpe if— No, how could she accuse her of anything so terrible? It would be most shameful if Kate were wrong, which she must be.

It did not help Kate's feelings, trying to remain generous and just to Miss Thorpe, to hear Julia in the process of abusing the fête to Mrs. Gresham.

"A dreary affair," she said, "even the lemonade has gone bad." She sniffed with disdain, setting down her cup.

"What utter nonsense." Kate was quick to spring to the defense. "Lemonade going bad? I never heard of such a thing."

"Taste it for yourself," Julia said with a shrug.

Kate stalked over and poured herself a cup. With the first sip, she nigh choked. It did indeed have a most peculiarly bitter flavor, but she would have choked even more before admitting such a thing to Julia.

"There is nothing in the least wrong with it." She forced down another swallow.

Julia's mouth pursed in annoyance. "My dearest

Kate, there is something gravely amiss with your sense of taste."

She raised her cup and took another drink. "Ugh, nasty."

In pure defiance, Kate downed the entire contents of her own, if only to prove how mistaken Julia was. Soon the other ladies were drawn into the dispute. After swallowing a glassful, Mrs. Gresham sputtered and ranged herself on Miss Thorpe's side. Mrs. Towers, although she puckered at her first mouthful, agreed quite loyally with Kate. The women continued to sip, argue, refill their cups and argue some more.

By her third glassful, Kate began to feel rather strange. Her fingers were going numb, but the most delightful tingly sensations rushed through her veins, making her feel quite light in the head. The quarrel started to seem not only downright silly, but the most amusing thing she had ever heard.

When Julia swayed, trying to say "purr-perfecktly dretful" and could not get it out, Kate clapped a hand to her mouth.

A high pitched giggle escaped her that she scarce recognized as her own.

Harry handed out the last of the prizes, a new cloak of gray worsted to the burly youth who had won the final race. He smiled vacantly while he glanced about him. Where was Kate? After all her anxiety, she had not come to watch any of the games. Nor had many of the other ladies. Perhaps the heat was proving too much for them. The sun blazing down on his head was certainly beginning to make him feel a little irritable.

He had not even had a chance to tell Kate that Mr. Ffolliot and Lord Erwin had departed with as much haste as they had arrived. Folly had slunk away, scarce taking time to bid farewell, looking more guilty than a pickpocket caught with his hand inside a lady's reticule. Harry had been too relieved by the departure to wonder overmuch at such odd behavior. He was sorry to see Ffolliot so much in Erwin's company. Perhaps at some later date, he could make an effort to persuade Folly—

A reluctant grin escaped Harry. He was indeed far gone if he planned to begin preaching reformation to others. What would the governor have thought!

So far the fête had been an unqualified success. But as the hour for the supper approached, Harry began to get a little anxious. He never had been much good sorting out ranks or who should be escorting whom into dinner. Where was Kate?

Harry's mind was not eased by the sight of Gravshaw approaching him. The man appeared uncommonly flustered, his coattails flapping behind him in a most unbutlerlike fashion. Harry grimaced. Flying into a pelter was getting to be an infernally bad habit with his once indomitable servant.

"Oh, my lord. You must come at once."

"Now what? Has one of the kitchen boys dropped the custards?"

"No, my lord." Gravshaw bent forward and mumbled something about grave crisis and ladies in the tent.

"What sort of crisis?" Harry drawled. "Are they in danger of bringing the contraption tumbling about their ears?"

"It wouldn't surprise me, sir."

"What?!"

Gravshaw pokered up, refusing to say more, glancing about him as though fearful of being overheard. With an exasperated sigh, Harry motioned him off, falling into step behind, feeling a little impatient of having to deal with another tempest in a teapot. Where the deuce was Kate?

"There, my lord." Gravshaw pointed at the tent

flap with a trembling finger. "Never in all my days as—"

"Oh, stubble it, Gravshaw. I get enough high drama from Lady Lytton without . . ."

Harry trailed off, startled by the sound that suddenly rang out from the tent, laughter, but not the well-bred mirth to be expected from ladies of quality. It sounded more like some doxies on a drunken spree.

He darted a questioning look at Gravshaw who stared stolidly ahead of him. Harry entered the tent with the butler creeping at his heels. Before Harry had time to so much as blink, a flash of silver came hurtling at him. A lady's sandal glanced off his chest and landed at his feet.

Startled, Harry tracked the missile to its owner. Julia leaned against Mrs. Gresham, the squire's wife providing none too steady support as Julia struggled to remove her other shoe.

"Gravshaw!" she barked. "You rashcal. Dinnit I bid you fetch some champagne?"

Harry's jaw went slack, the flushed blowsy-looking woman scarcely resembling the icy perfection that was Julia Thorpe. Her unfocused blue eyes drifted toward him and she hiccuped.

"Good. Here's Lytton. He'll make that villain obey."

Mrs. Gresham tittered. She ogled Harry and slurred, "I do love this fashion for tight breeches." She whispered something to Kate's mama and both women went off into a fit of that disconcerting laughter.

Damnation! If Harry had not known better, he would have said they were all as well glazed as a parcel of sailors on shore leave. In the midst of this madness, it was a great relief to see Kate seated calmly on a stool. Harry hastened over to her.

"Kate, what's wrong with your mother and Julia?"

She glanced up slowly, a beatific smile spreading over her face.

"Harry!" Kate swayed to her feet, and if Harry had not caught her, she would have tumbled to the ground. She merely giggled, wrapping her arms around his neck. Harry inhaled an unmistakable odor.

"Gin!" he cried, outraged. "Gravshaw, what the devil have you been feeding these women?"

" 'Twasn't me, my lord. I came into the tent earlier and . . . and I greatly fear your friend Lord Erwin did something to the lemonade."

"Ridiculous," Kate said. "Nothing wrong with the lemonade." She clung to him, allowing her weight to sag against his frame, nearly tipping Harry off balance. Harry cursed Erwin under his breath, his mind filling with a vision of what he would do with the bounder the next time he laid eyes upon him.

"To hell with lemonade," Julia called out. "We want champagne. Go fetch it." She gave Gravshaw a ringing smack on his rump.

The butler appeared about to have a fit of apoplexy at this affront to his dignity. As appalling as the situation was, Harry's chest rumbled with the desire to laugh. But it was nigh impossible to do so with Kate maintaining such a stranglehold on his neck. He managed to gasp. "Fetch water, Gravshaw, at once."

"Why?" The squire's wife trilled. "Is someone about to deliver a babe?"

Her comment provoked another gale of hysterical laughter.

"*Cold* water, Gravshaw," Harry shouted above the din. The butler looked only too relieved to scurry from the tent.

Harry tried to ease Kate away, but she hugged him tighter. "Schtop giving so many silly orders and kiss me, you foolish boy."

"Kate . . . Kate! Behave yourself and sit down."

"I am behaving very badly, aren't I?"

"Yes, you are," Harry said with all the gravity he could muster.

" 'Tis great fun." She chuckled, then stood on tiptoe until she brushed the tip of her small nose against his. She stared owlishly into his eyes. "Harry, I . . . I don't know how. But I think I may have shot the dog."

"I fear you have, love." Harry regarded her with tender amusement. She wriggled out of his arms. Although somewhat unsteady, she managed to keep her feet.

"Need some air. Need to find Mrs. Prangle."

"No!" Harry cut her off in alarm. "Believe me, Kate, this is not the time to go seeking out the archdeacon's wife."

To his relief, she nestled quite contentedly back into his embrace. Harry felt beads of perspiration gather on his brow. This was the most damnable coil he had ever found himself in. If he did not wish this day to end in complete disgrace and scandal, he had to keep all these women confined to the tent until they could be brought to some state of sobriety.

"Ladies, please. All of you sit down," he commanded. "We're going to have some tea."

"Tea be damned," the incorrigible Julia shrilled, shying her other sandal at him. "Bring us the bloody champagne."

While Harry wondered where Julia had ever acquired such language, Kate looked up at him, breathless with laughter. "You are so 'dorable, Harry, when you try to be stern. I do love you. I will never be vexed with you again."

"You will, my dear. Oh, yes, you will," he muttered. The next minutes that stretched out proved more nervewracking than those hours spent waiting the enemy's charge at Waterloo. Harry would have defied Wellington himself to keep order amid a parcel of very foxed ladies.

Mrs. Gresham nearly drew his cork, attempting to leave the tent, shrieking she was being held prisoner. Julia leaped up the table, declaring that it was "Better to marry, than to burn," and launched into a sermon threatening him with fire and brimstone.

As for Kate, she began nuzzling kisses beneath his ear in a manner that was painfully distracting, while Mrs. Towers hummed quietly to herself. When Harry heard someone at the flap, he gasped, "Gravshaw, thank God."

But his prayer of gratitude was cut short. Instead of the butler, it was Reverend Thorpe that peeked into the tent.

If Harry could have done so, he would have thrust Adolphus right back out, but any such maneuver was impossible with Kate melting against him.

"My lord! Miss Towers!" The vicar's eyes popped with disapproval.

"Hell and damnation!" Julia cried with a sweeping flourish of her hand.

Adolphus's shocked gaze swiveled to his sister. "Julia!"

"We all know our names," Harry snapped. "Would you kindly do something useful like getting your sister down from there and, oh damn—"

While Harry's attention had been fixed on Adolphus, the squire's wife had managed to escape from the tent. As soon as Mrs. Gresham staggered out, Lady Dane stalked in.

"What is going on in here, Lytton?" she demanded.

Harry groaned, feeling the entire situation slipping beyond his control. As the vicar tugged Julia down from her perch, she burst into tears, wailing, "Oh, why wasn't I born a man?"

Even the gentle Mrs. Towers joined the fracas, tipsily shaking her finger at Lady Dane. "You're a mos' tiresome, meddlin' old woman. Hold your tongue and stop orderin' everyone about."

Harry was not privileged to hear Lady Dane's shocked response, for his attention was claimed by a bellow of outrage from outside the tent. Apparently, the squire had just encountered his wife. Harry rolled his eyes, not able to imagine how this horrific scene could possibly get any worse when he felt a tug at his sleeve.

He glanced down to discover Kate's face gone alarmingly pale.

"Oh, Harry," she said. "I . . . I think I'm going to be sick."

Chapter 11

The day after the fête, morning dawned just as bright and clear, but Kate made no movement to bound out of bed. She lay flat on her back, the light striking against her eyelids only served to intensify the throbbing in her head.

Merciful heavens! If she had been a condemned prisoner, she would have begged the executioner to wield his ax. Amputation was surely the only cure for such agony.

By degrees, she came more fully awake and attempted to roll onto her side. A soft moan escaped her, her stomach muscles feeling bruised and sore. Her mind yet hazed with pain and sleep, Kate tried to recollect the reason for her wretched state. What sort of mishap had befallen her? What dread manner of illness?

She forced her eyes open. The room pitched so precariously, she had to close them. Raising her lids just a fraction, she managed to focus, peering at her room through the thickness of her lashes.

The chamber appeared as ever a haven of serenity and order except for the frock crumpled upon the carpet, the same frock she had worn yesterday when she had—

Kate sucked in her breath as memory flooded back

to her. Harry, the fête ... the lemonade! She groaned, flinging one arm across her eyes as though that gesture might serve to shut out the remembrance. But recollections, at first quite fuzzy, began to emerge with painful clarity.

She had been arguing with Miss Thorpe about the lemonade. Why had she not paid more heed to Julia's insistence that something was wrong? The vicar's sister had been odiously correct. Kate vaguely recalled Harry's conversation with his butler, something about Harry's horrid friend, Lord Erwin, tampering with the punch bowl. He had added ... what was it Harry had exclaimed?

Gin! That was it. Dear Lord! She had been gulping down gin. How oft she had heard Papa preach against that evil brew—the bane of the poorer classes the bishop had called it. What would he have said if he had seen its effect upon his own daughter?

Kate could not say precisely all that she had done, but she knew, with dread certainty, she had been thoroughly intoxicated. Groaning, she massaged her throbbing temples, seeking to recall what was best forgotten.

The laughter ... everything had seemed so uproariously amusing. And Harry ... she had flirted with him. Flirted! Kate winced. Nay, she had pounced upon him in a manner that would have shamed a tavern wench. He had attempted to make her sit down, but she had kept right on kissing him before the entire assemblage of other ladies.

Kate's cheeks burned at the memory. And then ... oh, no. Had the vicar really come into the tent? And Grandmama? She could not be sure for at that point Harry had helped her back to the house because suddenly all had no longer been so diverting.

Kate half pulled the counterpane over her head as she remembered the gleaming white chamber pot, Harry's strong arm supporting her while she had been hideously sick. After that, all was blank. She had no idea when she had been conveyed home or how she had come to be tucked up in her bed.

It scarce mattered, she thought, her face damp with humiliation. One fact emerged with painful clarity. She had made an utter fool of herself. She would never be able to face anyone in Lytton's Dene again—especially not Harry.

It afforded her no consolation that she had not been alone in her folly. Julia, the squire's wife, and . . . and Mama! Kate bolted to a sitting position, the sudden movement making her head feel as though an anvil had clanged down upon it. But the pain was as nothing placed beside the horrified remembrance. Mama, too, had drunk of that poisonous concoction. If Kate had been rendered so deathly ill, what had it done to one of Mrs. Towers's delicate constitution?

Thoroughly alarmed, Kate flung back the covers. Although her stomach did a series of flip-flops, she managed to stand. Never sure how she accomplished it, she crossed to the washstand and sloshed some water from the pitcher into the basin.

The chill liquid stung her flesh, but it revived her enough that she could struggle into her silk wrapper and mules. Padding down the hallway to her mother's room, Kate did not even pause to knock. She thrust the portal open, expecting to find Mrs. Towers at death's door.

But the rose-colored chamber was empty, the bed already made, the shawl Mrs. Towers habitually wore missing from its peg. Far from being reassured, Kate stumbled from the room toward the stairway. She started down, grimacing at every step. Why had she never noticed before how badly each riser creaked?

At the bottom, she nearly collided with Mollie, the plump maid bustling from the small dining room with empty plates. Kate took one look at the china greasy with the remnants of egg and broiled kidney. She shuddered, clutching her hand to her stomach.

"Good morning, miss," Mollie said cheerfully, the scarlet ribbons on her mobcap fluttering in a perky fashion that seemed an affront to Kate's eyes.

Kate stared fixedly at a point past the offending crockery and the ribbons. "Where is my mother?" she rasped.

"Why, gone out, miss, with Lady Dane, to take a turn about the garden out back."

"Mama is . . . is out *walking*?"

"Yes, miss. She and her ladyship have already breakfasted and said as how you were not to be disturbed."

Kate scarce heard the girl, her mind reeling with relief and confusion. How was it possible? Mama had drunk at least as much of the lemonade as she, hadn't she? Obviously her memory was none too clear.

"Are you all right, miss?" Mollie asked, peering closely at Kate. "Will you be wanting your breakfast now? There is none of the kidney left, but I believe Cook has some kippers—"

Kate took a deep gulp. "Just a little weak tea, please."

Motioning Mollie to remove the congealing dishes from her sight, Kate leaned up against the oak banister. She could not quite face the prospect of mounting the stairs again, so she retired to the parlor. They would not be likely to have any callers at this hour and, in any event, Kate never intended to receive anyone for the rest of her life.

Within the parlor, she drew the drapes across the bow window, shutting out as much of the sun as she could. Not only was the funereal gloom more soothing to her eyes, but it cast Papa's portrait into shadows, preventing the bishop's stern gaze from glaring down upon her disgrace.

Mollie bustled in and settled a tray near where Kate collapsed onto the settee. After much ruthless rattling of the teaspoons and the cup and saucer, the girl finally left Kate to sip her tea in merciful silence. The brew fortified her somewhat, but she could do naught to dispel the overwhelming burden of shame weighing down upon her.

When Kate heard a muffled sound that told her of an arrival in the hall beyond, she shrank down against the cushions. In her current state, she was uncertain she could even confront her own mama and grandmother.

But the rumble of voices that followed sent a shaft of uneasiness through her. That did not sound like Mama.

Mollie poked her head in the door and announced with a pert grin. "Beg pardon, miss. What should I do? Lord Lytton is here, and he threatens to cut off my cap ribbons if I don't—"

"No!" Kate bolted to her feet, her cup and saucer clattering to the carpet. "Send him away! Tell him I am sick, dead, gone on a long voyage."

"Perhaps you had best tell me yourself." Harry squeezed past Mollie, regarding Kate with a quizzical gleam in his eye. He had obviously taken great pains with his appearance, looking almost irritatingly handsome and full of vigor in his crisp, navy frock coat and whipcord breeches.

He thrust the highly interested Mollie out of the parlor and closed the door. Kate spun away from him, one hand fluttering with dismay to the disheveled curls tumbling about her shoulders, the other clutching at the neckline of her wrapper.

"My lord, you . . . you can see I am in no fit state to entertain visitors."

"You look as lovely as always, although more pale than I could wish." She heard the tread of his boots as he stepped beside her, stroking back her hair.

Even that featherlight touch caused her to tremble.

"My poor darling." Harry's voice rumbled sympathy close to her ear. "You must have had a very devil of a night. You ought to be taking something more than tea. Believe me, I have had ... er ... a little experience in these matters."

"Oh, Harry, please! Please just go away." Her voice broke and she retreated toward the window, burying her face in her hands.

"Kate!" He followed her. Placing his hands upon her shoulders, he tried to bring her about. She twisted away from him sinking down upon the windowseat. But there was no escape. With tender persistence, he hunkered down before her, gently forcing down her hands, gathering them into the strength of his own.

Tears gathered in her eyes, one escaping to trickle past her nose. "Please," she whispered. "Don't look at me. I am so ashamed."

He caught the tear, one rough fingertip brushing it aside. "Kate, dearest, you've naught to be ashamed of."

"Indeed I have. My behavior yesterday—"

" 'Twas no fault of yours."

"M-my conduct was dreadful, and the fête was r-ruined."

"It was nothing of the kind. We still contrived to hold the supper after I had sent you home. I told everyone you had been taken ill, and, hang it all, Kate! Don't cry." He intercepted another tear. "You know I can endure anything but that."

But now that she had begun, Kate could not check the flow, though the release of the emotion brought no comfort, only increasing the pounding tempo in her head.

Harry squeezed her hands. "Devil take that villain Erwin," he muttered. "Damned if I don't call him out for this."

His words sparked a bitter anger in Kate, as un-expected as it was unreasoning. She wrenched her hands away. "Aye, isn't that just a man's solution to everything. Blow a hole in someone, and that will mend matters at once."

Harry frowned, straightened slowly to his feet. "What would you have me do, Kate?"

"There's nothing you can do." Leaping up, she brushed past him, swiping at her eyes. "The damage is quite done."

"You might be interested to know that I discovered who purloined that invitation and posted it. It was your good friend, Julia Thorpe."

Kate started only a little to hear her worst suspicions confirmed. "What odds does that make? It was *your* friends who put the gin in the lemonade and . . . and you promised you would not let them do anything to spoil the fête."

Her voice sounded childishly petulant and, deep in her heart, Kate knew she was being unfair. But her head ached so abominably, she wanted to scream.

"I did my best, Kate," Harry said. She heard him sigh as though regathering the ends of his patience.

He approached again, making one more effort to ease her into his embrace. She backed away, and his arms dropped to his sides, a hint of exasperation in his voice. "You are making far too great a piece of work over all this, Kate. No one else is taking it so seriously, I warrant you."

He could not have said anything less calculated to soothe her. She was miserable, about to perish from humiliation, and no one regarded it seriously?

Harry plunged on, making bad worse. "By the end of the day, the squire was laughing over the affair and even Adolphus was most understanding."

"That is all very well for them," Kate said. "But I assure you my father would not have been amused.

It might be thought tolerable for a squire's wife to become drunk on gin, but . . . but—"

"But you are a bishop's daughter," Harry finished bitterly. "I fear I had allowed myself to forget that."

"So did I! Every time I am with you, I end up in the most improper—" She broke off clutching her head, which felt nigh ready to burst. "Please . . . please, can you not just leave me alone?"

A heavy silence ensued, then Harry said softly, "Yes, I rather think that it would be better if I did."

There was no rancor in his tones. He sounded so subdued that, despite her own agony, Kate glanced up at him. He looked neither angry nor even irritated, those expressive green eyes frighteningly empty. The powerful set of his shoulders slumped as in defeat.

As he moved toward the door, Kate half whispered, "Harry." If he heard her, he pretended otherwise. He bade her farewell, his parting adieu brief, sad, and heartbreakingly final.

Then he was gone.

Kate kept to her room for the rest of the day. By the next afternoon, she continued to send down her excuses, declining to join Mrs. Towers and Lady Dane for luncheon.

The meal was a simple one, consisting mostly of cold meats and fruit. Mrs. Towers picked at a few grapes. Although she had not fared as badly as Kate from the lemonade episode, she bore little appetite, being consumed by worry about her daughter.

Yet she put on a placid front, unwilling to admit as much to Lady Dane. That formidable dame was far too quick to criticize her precious Kate. At the opposite end of the linen tablecloth, her ladyship tapped her fork irritably against the crystal.

"How long is this nonsense going to continue?" she said presently.

"What nonsense is that, Mother Towers?"

"You know full well what I mean—this sorry business of Kate hiding out in her room."

"The child has been ill."

"Humpfh! Just the same as that Thorpe chit has been ill?"

Mrs. Towers winced. Lady Dane's acid comment referred to the visit the vicar had paid earlier that morning. Reverend Thorpe had come by to convey Julia's farewell to Kate. It seemed Miss Thorpe was journeying up north to stay with an elderly aunt in Scotland, "for reasons of Julia's health."

"Running away—that is what Julia Thorpe is doing," Lady Dane continued, slamming her fork down. "I would have hoped that a granddaughter of mine would have more bottom than that."

"So Kate does. She will come out when she is ready," Mrs. Towers said, although she was not sure herself. What a cruel contrast it was. Kate had been so sunny and smiling the morning of the fête. It seemed Lady Dane's interference might have done some good after all. Mrs. Towers had been certain that her daughter's most unusual courtship with Lord Lytton was about to be brought to a happy conclusion. Then that disaster in the tent! Mrs. Towers had wracked her mind ever since wondering if there was something she could have done to prevent it. If only she had not been so quick to agree with Kate about the lemonade.

These tormenting reflections were interrupted by Lady Dane. With a mighty scowl, she said, "I hope you have noticed that Lytton has not been back since we saw him ride off so hurriedly yesterday morn. I have had no chance to speak with him, but it is my belief that foolish child has sent him away again."

She flung her napkin down, scraping her chair back. Leaning on her cane, she rose, the familiar martial light coming to her eye. "I can see 'tis more than time I shook some sense into Kathryn."

Mrs. Towers believed that the last thing Kate needed was more of her grandmother's bullying. "I wish you would not."

As Lady Dane ignored her, stalking toward the door, Mrs. Towers hastened to intercept her. Although she trembled a little, she planted herself in front of her ladyship.

"I . . . I thought I had made my feelings clear to you before—"

"So you did, Maisie. You said a good many disagreeable things in your state of intoxication. However I realize you were not yourself, so I am disposed to pardon you."

"I was not that drunk."

Mrs. Towers's admission seemed to crack through the room with all the force of a thunderclap. Lady Dane was stunned into a rare moment of silence. Mrs. Towers's courage nigh failed her, but she realized she had already passed the point of no return.

"I . . . I do not think your meddling has always done Kate good, my lady. And . . . and I forbid any more of it."

This last she said so quietly, Lady Dane had to bend slightly to catch it. As she drew herself up stiffly, Mrs. Towers half expected to be struck aside by her ladyship's cane.

"And what pray tell do you intend to do?" Lady Dane demanded. "Allow the girl to remain closeted abovestairs until the end of her days?"

"No. I intend to speak to Kate myself."

An amused expression crossed Lady Dane's features, like a mighty eagle hearing a sparrow offering to take over the task of seeking out prey.

"Then I suggest you get about it before Kate takes to wearing hair shirts as well." Her ladyship stalked to the door and opened it for Mrs. Towers. Lady

Dane, of course, did not smirk, but the expression on her face was akin to it.

Mrs. Towers had little choice but to accept the challenge. Gathering up her dignity, she rustled past. With Lady Dane's fierce gaze upon her, she mounted the stairs to the second floor, her heart fluttering with trepidation. She had never borne any influence with Kate before. What on earth was she going to say to her daughter now?

At her timid knock upon the bedchamber door, Kate's lackluster voice bade her enter. She stepped inside the chamber to discover Kate seated upon a low stool by the fireside. She was bent industriously over a tambour frame, although Mrs. Towers had a strong suspicion the embroidery had only been snatched up with her entrance.

Kate glanced up, her appearance neat and trim, but her wan smile and the hollows beneath her eyes were enough to break Mrs. Towers's heart. "Mama! I thought you would be taking your nap."

"Not this afternoon, dear." Mrs. Towers closed the door behind her. "I came to see how you were feeling."

"A little better," Kate said with forced cheerfulness. She ducked her head, concentrating on her needle. Mrs. Towers noted that the delicate stitching had not progressed much from when she had last seen the work in Kate's hand. Gently, she removed the frame from her daughter's grasp.

"I think it is time you got out a little."

Kate flinched with dismay. "Oh, no, truly, Mama. You must not worry about me."

It was the old evasion, but this time Mrs. Towers knew she could not accept it. She caught Kate's face between her hands so that she could look into her troubled eyes.

"Worrying is a mother's prerogative, Kathryn. Now tell me what is wrong."

"N-nothing." Kate gave an overbright smile.

"I don't believe you," Mrs. Towers said. "The day of the fête I nigh expected Lord Harry to ask permission to pay his addresses."

"Harry would never have thought of anything like that and c-certainly not now that I—" Her eyes filled with tears and suddenly she cupped Mrs. Towers's hand, holding it to her cheek. "Oh, Mama, I am s-so unhappy, I just want to die."

She broke down completely, weeping. Mrs. Towers plunked down upon the carpet, her skirts billowing about her, gathering Kate into her arms as though she had been all of six years old.

"N-no, Mama," Kate sobbed against her shoulder. "I—I shouldn't burden you."

"Of course, you should," Mrs. Towers said, her own throat constricting. "Please. Tell mama what is hurting you."

It was a most foolish thing to say, as though Kate were yet a babe with naught but a skinned elbow. But her daughter nestled closer, entwining her arms about Mrs. Towers's neck. Maisie Towers closed her eyes, briefly recalling all those times she had allowed Kate to be borne away by the nurse or the governess for "the sake of Mrs. Towers's delicate health."

To have Kate at last turning to her for comfort was most bittersweet.

Kate's words came haltingly, but gradually she poured out the entire story of her quarrel with Lord Lytton. "And . . . and I know I was being most unjust to b-blame him, but he should have seen how miserable I was. Th-then I just let him go. I suppose 'tis . . . 'tis just as well."

"Why, darling?" Mrs. Towers murmured against her daughter's silky curls. "If you love him—"

"But Papa always said we would never suit. You know he did."

Mrs. Towers sighed. "The bishop was full of wisdom, but sometimes even the most clever men are less than wise when dealing with their daughters. I always thought your Papa a shade overprotective. I oft wondered whom he would have considered good enough to wed you."

Kate drew away, regarding her with surprise. "But surely, Mama, Papa's fears were justified. Harry's reputation was so shocking. Marrying him would have been a great risk."

"Any marriage is a risk. Your Papa and I went through quite a period of adjustment in our early days."

Kate's tear drenched eyes widened. "But Papa was never wild like Harry."

A gentle laugh escaped Mrs. Towers. "Well, I do recall him telling me about a time before he had taken holy orders, one Season when he went up to London. I fear he did some things that were quite scandalous for a future bishop."

"Papa?" Kate gasped.

Mrs. Towers nodded, although she could not quite meet her daughter's eye.

"But he always seemed so perfect," Kate said.

"He tried to be, perhaps rather too hard." Mrs. Towers smoothed a stray curl from Kate's petal-soft cheek. " 'Tis a failing I fear you often share, my dearest Kate."

Kate's blush acknowledged the fact, her lips parting in a rueful smile.

"Now, if you love your Harry as much as I think you do, you had best be giving him another chance."

Kate's smile quickly faded. "I fear this time he has given up on me, Mama. He has asked me to marry him so many times. I . . . I do not think he will be asking again."

"Then you must ask him."

"Mama!"

"There are ways, Kathryn, that a lady may arrange her proposal without being unmaidenly."

They regarded each other for a moment, then Kate flung her arms about Mrs. Towers in a brisk hug, with a conspiratorial laugh that only two women could share.

Mrs. Towers got to her feet, wincing at the stiffness in her joints. She was getting a little old for sitting upon the carpet. Shuffling toward the door, she took affectionate leave of her daughter.

She had no notion if her words had had any lasting effect upon the child, but as she closed the door, Kate's eyes looked soft and luminous, the set of her brow extremely thoughtful.

Mrs. Towers sighed. She had come to this mothering business rather late in her life. It was not simple by any means. She could only hope she had made an adequate job of it.

As Kate fetched her cloak from the wardrobe, she felt suffused with a warm glow from the recent scene with her mother. It was most strange how one could live in the same house with one's parents for so many years and not truly know either of them.

It saddened her to think, having at last become better acquainted with Mama, she was now thinking of leaving her. Of course, that rather depended on Harry.

Kate stopped in the act of swirling her cloak about her shoulders, her courage nigh failing her. But she forced her fingers into brisk movement, fastening the braided frogs. Then she bolted from her chamber and down the steps lest she lose heart and change her mind.

For the bishop's daughter was planning to do a very shocking thing. She proposed to call upon a gentleman, completely unchaperoned, without even a maid in attendance. Stepping round to the small coach house behind the cottage, Kate had the Towers' groom hitch the pony to the cart.

In less than half an hour, she was tooling along the lane with all the expertise Harry had taught her. She cast an anxious glance skyward, the succession of bright days quite fled before the gray clouds gathering. She trusted she would manage to reach Mapleshade before the rain broke.

Passing through the village did not prove the ordeal Kate had once anticipated in the privacy of her room. No one regarded her as an anathema, Miss Lethbridge even cheerily waving her handkerchief from the door of her shop. It was a little difficult when she passed the squire on horseback and he shot her a knowing grin. Kate merely blushed and did not attempt to climb beneath the cart seat as she would like to have done.

As she clattered between the great iron gates and down the winding drive, Mapleshade's familiar red brick greeted her, rather solemn and subdued beneath the overcast sky. One of Harry's efficient grooms came promptly to take charge of the pony cart and Kate was left facing the tall pillars, the whitewashed stairs leading to the imposing front door.

She moistened her lips nervously. Suppose . . . suppose Harry refused to see her. She had denied being at home to him often enough. Taking a deep breath to calm her wildly thudding heart, Kate marched forward and seized the huge brass knocker.

Her summons was so timid, she wondered if anyone could have heard it, but the door swung open promptly, not answered by one of the footmen, but by Gravshaw himself.

Remembering the last circumstances under which Harry's butler had seen her, Kate squirmed, unable to look past that redoubtable manservant's starched waistcoat.

"Miss Towers! Thank God you have come!"

The fervent greeting was so unlike the scornful disapproval Kate expected, she glanced up. The butler looked quite distraught.

As Kate stepped past him into the marble tiled hall, apprehension clutched at her heart. "Is something wrong, Gravshaw?" she asked. "Pray, tell me. N-nothing has happened to Lord Lytton?"

"No, miss. That is, I trust not."

What did he mean he trusted not! Kate's fingers froze in the action of being about to remove her cloak. "What is it? What is amiss?"

"We are all at sixes and sevens here, Miss Towers, and that's the truth." His features contorted, and Kate could tell that he struggled with that natural reserve that prevented the elderly retainer from discussing the family with strangers. But it seemed a long time since Kate had been considered an outsider at Mapleshade.

" 'Tis Lady Lytton," he continued in a rush. "She . . . she . . . *She has eloped with that Crosbie fellow.*"

"Dear heavens! Are you certain?"

"Yes, miss. Yesterday afternoon her ladyship ordered up her coach to go into the village. I thought it a little odd, for as you know, she never does so. By supper she had not returned and Lord Lytton found a note in her sitting room."

The elderly butler shook his head. "There is no doubt, miss. The countess has most certainly run off."

Kate bit down upon her lip. "And Harry—I mean Lord Lytton. What was his response to all this?" she asked, nigh dreading Gravshaw's answer.

"He rode out looking for her ladyship at once. The master searched all night, but he could not overtake her."

Kate sighed with relief, at least rid of the apprehension of Harry being hung for the murder of poor Mr. Crosbie.

"Where is his lordship now?"

"He took his horse into the stables about an hour ago and then just walked off. No one quite knows where he went." Graveshaw's chin trembled. "The young master has taken all this very badly, Miss Towers. You see he was her ladyship's trustee. According to his father's will—"

"I understand all that, Gravshaw, but you must not worry." She added softly, "I think I know exactly where his lordship has gone."

Kate had not been nigh Harry's Hill his since the day of the memorial service. Hitching up her skirts, she labored up the slope, peering at the distant summit. The Hill was a bleak place on this chill autumn day, scatterings of dead leaves whisking by on the wind, Harry's memorial appearing abandoned and forgotten.

The site bore an aura of loneliness about it, a desolation that seemed centered in the man who hunched on the statue's base. Harry sat with his chin propped on his hand, staring vacantly across the sweep of his land, the woods with their half-bared branches stark against the leaden gray sky.

As she drew closer, Kate marked the unshaven line of his jaw, the shadows darkening eyes dulled from lack of sleep. He seemed so pulled down, Kate could scarce curb the impulse to fling her arms about him and cradle his weary head against her breast. But she hesitated, uncertain of her reception.

Harry did not notice her approach until she stood close enough that she could have stroked back the unruly dark strands the wind whipped across his brow. When he finally did glance up, his only reaction was one of mild surprise.

None of the joy that usually lit up his eyes at the sight of her, no uttering of her name with unbounded delight, not a hint of that lightning smile. To Kate, it was as though the sun had indeed gone out of the world.

"H-hello, Harry," she said.

He bestirred himself, stretching his long limbs as he rose stiffly to his feet. "Miss Towers." He sketched a brief bow.

Kate's heart sank. This was going to be worse than she had thought. Giving him no chance to question her sudden appearance, she blurted out. "I . . . I have been calling down at the house. I heard about Lady Lytton."

Harry grimaced. "I dare say everyone will have by the time the day is out. It should provide more entertainment than the most roaring farce." Kate thought she had never heard his voice laced with such bitterness.

He sneered. "Hellfire Harry for once tries to play propriety and keep his stepmother from making a fool of herself, but can't quite manage it." He expelled his breath in a deep sigh. "Damn! But that should come as no surprise to you. I never do seem to do anything right."

Kate wished she could caress him under the chin, saying as he had done so many times to her. "You are taking this all too seriously, Harry."

Instead she stood awkwardly, shuffling her feet. " 'Tis pity it had to come to this. But I fear the elopement was partly my fault."

"Yours?"

Although she shrank from his hard stare, she explained, "I promised Mr. Crosbie and Lady Lytton I would speak to you the day of the fête about their engagement. When I didn't quite get to it, I fear they became desperate."

"You were going to act as . . . as emissary for that fortune hunter?" Harry did not appear angry so much as incredulous.

"I believe he truly loves her. Why, the elopement

itself makes it obvious Mr. Crosbie cares not for your threat to cut off her ladyship's allowance."

"Even if that were true, 'tis a damned ridiculous match. He's a simpleton, and as for her! There has to be at least twenty years difference in their ages."

Kate stared at the ground for a moment, then gathering her courage, she said, "I have had much time to think these past few days. My belief is when two people are truly in love, all those differences in age, station, and family simply don't matter." She dared to look deep into Harry's eyes, hoping he would understand what she was trying to tell him, that she was speaking of far more than Lady Lytton and Mr. Crosbie.

But Harry looked away from her, the muscles along his jaw inflexible. "You don't understand at all, Kate. My father gave me the responsibility—"

"Of managing Lady Lytton's money. But do you truly think he expected you to act as her chaperon for the rest of her life?"

"No, but—"

"Of course, I know how dreadfully you are going to miss her ladyship."

An unwilling choked sound came from Harry. Kate felt hope stir. She had nearly broken through his grim barrier, made him laugh.

She continued gently, "You have done wonderfully well with the trust your father left you. I am sure he would have been very proud."

"You think so? I begin to harbor the fear the governor would think I have been making a great cake of myself, especially over this business with Sybil." A rueful smile touched Harry's lips. "Likely he would be right."

He turned to Kate suddenly, his voice gone low, earnest. "I know the old earl had a dreadful reputation. But he wasn't a bad man, Kate. I still miss him.

Only there were occasions that I rather wished . . ." He hesitated. "I wished that he had been a little less my friend and a little more my father."

So rarely had Harry ever let his guard down, permitting her to see the pain, the more somber side of the handsome rakehell that Kate heard herself agreeing softly. "I know. There were times when I wished mine had been more my father and a little less the bishop."

This admission astonished her as much as it did Harry. Their eyes met and in that instant Kate felt they had acquired a deeper understanding of each other than they had ever known before.

He unfolded his arms and Kate held her breath, half expecting to be drawn into his embrace. But he merely shrugged, returning back to the subject of Lady Lytton. "I suppose I will have to make the best of the situation and receive Crosbie at Mapleshade as Sybil's husband. Just as long as he doesn't inflict any more of his damned sculpture upon me."

Harry tipped back his head, peering upward at the naked warrior that towered above them. "But I do intend to have that cursed thing carted off my hill as soon as may be."

"No, don't." Kate said. "I have rather grown to like it." Boldly she forced her gaze up that disturbingly lifelike representation of male flesh. She faltered, "Of course, perhaps we should contrive to get some clothes upon him."

Harry's laugh did boom out then, hearty and deep. Kate thought she could feel it ring in her heart.

"What I had better contrive," he said with a chuckle, "is to get you home before the storm breaks. I thought I heard a rumble of thunder."

He tucked her arm within his, with a return of that familiar heart-stopping smile. As they hastened down the hill, Kate's pulses raced with anticipation.

She was certain that at any moment he would ask her to marry him. Her answer, her lips, her heart were all eager and ready.

But to her confusion and dismay, Harry whisked her into his curricle and they were soon on the way back through the village. Thus far he had not said a word, at least none that she was longing to hear. He appeared to be taking great care to avoid any mention of their quarrel or the episode at the fête. With maddening cheerfulness, he chatted of the most insignificant matters.

Friends, Kate thought wretchedly. He now means for us to be no more than friends, just as she had always insisted. Would that someone had cut out her tongue.

By the time Harry deposited her at the cottage, Kate nigh trembled with her desperation. He did not even attempt to take her by the hand as he opened the gate for her.

"I am glad to see you are looking better than when we last met," he said.

"Yes." Kate agreed, regarding him hopefully. "Though I have decided I had better swear off the gin."

Her timid jest provoked a grin from him, but he made no movement to follow her inside the fence. To her acute dismay, he vaulted back into the seat of his curricle. Did he truly mean to leave without saying another word?

"Harry . . ." Kate began, then blushed. No, she could not do it. She could not be the one to ask him. Miserably, she stood, fidgeting with the latch on the gate.

"Good day to you, Miss Towers. My regards to your mother and Lady Dane." Harry gathered up the reins. He paused, adding somewhat wistfully. "I don't suppose you want to marry me, do you?"

"Oh, yes! Yes, I do." Kate cried out with joy and relief.

To her astonishment, he nodded glumly and set his horse into motion. Kate's jaw dropped for a moment, then she crowded close to the gate, watching in fascination, wondering how far he was going to get before her answer registered with him.

The curricle had not advanced as far as the turning in the lane, when Harry sawed back so ruthlessly on the reins, the horse reared in the traces. Kate realized that she must finally have been infected with his lordship's puckish sense of humor, for she took an unholy delight in observing how Hellfire Harry, that most notable of whips, became positively cowhanded in his frantic efforts to bring the curricle around.

As the vehicle thundered back to the gate, Harry almost leaped down before he brought the mare to a halt. He rushed panting to her side.

"Kate! What . . . what the devil did you just say?"

Laughter bubbled up inside her. "I said yes, you silly man. Yes, I want to marry you."

Harry let out a war whoop. Seizing her about the waist, he raised her up and spun her about until they were both light-headed and giddy with laughing.

Then slowly Harry lowered her to her feet, the laughter stilling, the expression in his eyes causing the breath to snag in her throat. He captured her lips with a hunger, a longing she felt strike deep to the core of her own heart. Crushing her hard against him, he kissed her with a most tender ruthlessness, until even the gray day about her spun bright with promise and sunshine.

"Kate, Kate." He murmured, a shudder coursing through his powerful frame. "You must know how I love you. How much I . . . I— Damn it, I meant to make a much better job of it this time."

"If you think you can do any better than this, my lord," she said huskily, the heat rushing through her veins. "I am certainly willing to let you try."

Seizing him by the collar, she brought his lips crashing down on hers again.

At the cottage's bow front window, the curtain stirred. Lady Dane peered out with a startled exclamation, then said tartly, "Maisie. Your daughter is making love to Lytton by the garden gate. I certainly hope this means they are betrothed."

Mrs. Towers joined her mother-in-law at the window. "I rather think it does," she said as she saw Kate locked in Harry's arms. The smile Mrs. Towers felt curve her lips was an odd mingling of joy, relief, and melancholy.

Her ladyship folded her arms in rigid silence. At last as though the words were fairly wrung from her, she said, "All right, Maisie, how did you do it? Whatever did you say to that stubborn child?"

"Nothing, truly. I just talked to Kate a little about her papa, told her some of the wild things he had done in his youth."

"Wild? My Dylan?" Lady Dane stared at Mrs. Towers as though she had run mad.

Mrs. Towers squirmed. "Well, he did tell me he went to London once. He actually lost two shillings at whist and . . . and permitted a woman of most doubtful reputation to speak to him."

"Why, Maisie Towers, you lied to the girl!"

"No, I didn't. I only exaggerated," Mrs. Towers murmured a little sheepishly. "Being only a bishop's wife and not his daughter, I am not quite burdened with as many scruples."

A glint of amusement and newfound respect appeared in Lady Dane's eyes. She gestured to where Kate and Harry lingered by the gate, yet lost to the world. "So what will you do now that you are about to part with your daughter?"

Mrs. Towers sighed. "I don't know. A small house in Yorkshire, perhaps with a hired companion. . . ."

Lady Dane cleared her throat. She said gruffly, "I don't suppose you would consider making your home with a most meddlesome and . . . and frequently lonely old woman?"

Despite her regal posture, there was a degree of humbleness in Lady Dane's request quite foreign to her nature.

After feigned consideration, Mrs. Towers replied, "I should be happy to come live with you."

Lady Dane seemed pleased, but so astonished by her response that Mrs. Towers hastened to explain. "You see, I know I would never have to have that dreadful Prangle woman into tea again."

Lady Dane laughed so hard, the sound carried even beyond the cottage walls. Kate caught sight of the pair at the window, and wondered what Mama could have said to occasion her ladyship such mirth. But even the knowledge she was being observed could not curb Kate's desire to have Harry kiss her again.

It was left to his lordship to playfully wag an admonishing finger at her. Then with a tender smile, he linked his arm through Kate's and they marched up the cottage path together to solicit her mother's blessing.

Regency Romance
at its finest...

MARION CHESNEY

Available at your bookstore or use this coupon.

____FIRST REBELLION	21631	$2.95
____FREDERICA IN FASHION	20585	$2.50
____GHOST AND LADY ALICE	21698	$2.95
____LADY MARGERY'S INTRIGUE	21659	$2.95
____MINERVA	20580	$2.25
____PAPER PRINCESS	21341	$2.95
____PERFECT GENTLEMAN	21342	$2.50
____SILKEN BONDS #2	21632	$3.50
____TAMING OF ANNABELLE	21457	$2.50

FAWCETT MAIL SALES
Dept. TAF, 201 E. 50th St., New York, N.Y. 10022

Please send me the FAWCETT BOOKS I have checked above. I am en-
closing $................(add $2.00 to cover postage and handling for the first
book and 50¢ each additional book). Send check or money order—no
cash or C.O.D.'s please. Prices are subject to change without notice.
Valid in U.S. only. All orders are subject to availability of books.

Name_____

Address_____

City_____State_____Zip Code_____

Allow at least 4 weeks for delivery.

14   TAF-26